UPPING THE STAKES

A NOVEL

CORINNE COLMAN

iUniverse LLC
Bloomington

UPPING THE STAKES

iUniverse books may be ordered through booksellers or by contacting:

iUniverse LLC
1663 Liberty Drive
Bloomington, IN 47403
www.iuniverse.com
1-800-Authors (1-800-288-4677)

ISBN: 978-1-4917-1984-8 (sc)
ISBN: 978-1-4917-1985-5 (e)

Library of Congress Control Number: 2013923532

Printed in the United States of America.

iUniverse rev. date: 04/03/2014

CHAPTER ONE

1980

The spirit of adventure was running high that cold January evening, speeding the bus over the bleak flatlands of New Jersey toward the lights towering in a glittering frieze across the black horizon.

A strong sea wind blew through the dim littered streets, but the darkness could not mask Atlantic City's plaintive shabbiness. Dilapidated frame houses, plastered with linoleum and boards lined the broken pavement. Tawdry bars and garish diners flickered red neon through the debris. In sharp contrast to the tattered streets, the chrome and glass hotel where I checked in that evening was alive with a stream of Saturday night arrivals.

The amplified shrieks of a rock band blasted through the cavernous casino, mingling with shouts, bells, the clanging of slot machines, the raucous screaming from the craps' tables and the wild clamor of excited crowds. The five-dollar blackjack tables were full but the desire to play irresistible. In an instant I was at a twenty-five dollar game.

Almost as quickly, the dealer admonished me for improper use of hand signals, revealing my status as Atlantic City neophyte.

A moment later, a tall attractive redhead sat down beside me. She wore a large diamond pin on the lapel of a black silk suit, an incongruous, amusing note of elegance in a denim and polyester crowd. Her long, blood red nails clicked rhythmically on the chips.

"How's this doll been treating you?" she asked, nodding toward the dealer.

"Too soon to tell," I said.

"We just got in about five minutes ago. My husband had a meeting so I escaped for a while," she said.

Dealt an ace and a three against the dealer's five, I hesitated.

"Double 'em," said the redhead quickly. "It's the right play."

Automatically following her advice, I won a large bet and we became friends.

"Thank you," I said, "I didn't know you could double that bet. It's not permitted in the Bahamas."

"Rules vary, Atlantic City's are different from the Bahamas and Las Vegas -- in Vegas the rules on the strip aren't the same as the big hotels. Glad to be of help. I'm Bonnie Fisher."

"Lily Jarman," I said, accepting her bejeweled hand.

"Your hands are shaking," she said.

"I'm nervous."

"Is this your first time in Atlantic City?"

"Yes."

"It's like coming home for me. I grew up in Freehold, New Jersey, about an hour away. We came down to the shore all the time when I was a kid." She paused and looked over at my cards. "Hey, you gotta great split going for you there. Bet it."

I made the bet and won again. "Where are you from, Lily?" Bonnie asked.

"New York City."

"Down here on your own?"

"Yes."

"Lucky you!" she said. "You can play to your heart's content. I'm crazy about my husband -- but not when I'm into blackjack."

Guided by the sure hand of my *cicerone*, I relaxed and enjoyed myself. Smoke swirled, drinks flowed, chips clicked and the band played, creating the illusion of a perpetual party. It was a great way to make money.

Bonnie's warmth and glamour were beguiling. Instructing me on basic strategy shoe after shoe, she was invaluable. Winning excited my imagination -- I sensed the possibility of being once more where I had been for so long -- on top of it all.

It was the dinner hour and the game belonged to the die-hards, those whose passion for gambling supersedes their need for food. Our group had become lively, filled with the music of gruff male voices and street accents. Taking advantage of the fact that we were the only women playing, Bonnie chatted up the men, made jokes and enlivened the scene with a stream of sexual innuendo. She flirted outrageously with the dealer, a shy, glossy-haired boy of Sicilian descent named Nino.

"There are more Italians here than in all of Italy," Bonnie said, "more even than Vegas. When I was in the chorus in Vegas, I had a guy that looked just like Nino, could've been his father. Hey, Nino, give me a blackjack. Now! You owe me babe!"

Bonnie, who had been playing one hundred a hand, suddenly bet all her money -- two tall stacks of chips, thousands of dollars. And in one of those lustrous moments of gambling's favor, she received the imperiously demanded blackjack. The table went wild and the men roared their approval.

"Ya gotta' scream for it. If you don't ask, you don't get nothin'," shouted one man.

"Ain't we lucky to be here!" said another.

"And we ain't never gonna leave!"

Bonnie tipped Nino grandly with a hundred-dollar chip. "Thank you, babe," she said. "What a win -- right on the money! I'm up fifteen thousand. I can't believe it. You're my lucky charm, Lily. I've got to keep you around. How you doing?"

"I'm ahead seven-hundred dollars," I said.

"Let's have a drink at the bar to celebrate. That's the move -- to leave while you're ahead. Now I should be able to play after dinner without any hassle from Sid. He thinks that gambling's only for fools and suckers. Not that he minds the money. He never begrudges me anything. The thing is, he works for the company that owns this hotel, and he hates the idea of me being hustled by his business associates. He also doesn't like the idea of my playing alone."

"Why?"

"It looks bad to the people who work for him. They're very into how things look. Sure, they want the casino overflowing, but not with family members."

In the bar we chose a table with a view of the passing parade. Bonnie ordered a scotch while I drank white wine.

"That blackjack was incredible," Bonnie said, "straight from heaven. And that dealer -- he's the spitting image of this guy Angelo who I hooked up with when I first hit Vegas. I was sixteen and trying to make it as a dancer. He was a struggling musician and between us, we didn't have a nickel. But what a passion! Fun and great in bed. Trouble is, he found his way into everyone else's bed, too."

Bonnie's voice assumed the husky tone women use when talking of past love. Her confidences didn't surprise me. The excitement of the moment released a flow of feeling. Motivated by the desire to confess after our win, personal reserve disappeared between us and bits of highly private history were traded in banter. Naked revelations, astonishing glimpses into the soul could be heard cheaply and examined greedily by strangers.

"By the time Angelo left," Bonnie said, "I was the head of the chorus. I had good times, sure, but life in Vegas is very hard.

Hard on the face and the body -- forget about the soul. You're old at twenty-five in the desert.

"Then, thank God, I met Sid, and presto, my whole life changed. We got married, moved to Los Angeles and became part of the world of big business. You know, charity benefits, beautiful people. We know everybody, go everywhere. We're at the right places at the right time. Beverly Hills, California -- it's a long way from Freehold, New Jersey."

"I've made that trip myself," I said.

"Yeah? Dressed up in your faded jeans and denim shirt and cowboy boots? Looking like money doesn't matter? You've *got* to be loaded. Am I right?"

"Almost right. I *was* loaded."

"What happened?"

"It's a long story."

And one, I thought, for which, despite my need to talk and unburden myself, I could find no words. There was only the image of us in the Bahamas, barely two weeks ago, glowing with health and sun, rising to the occasion of pleasure and the greater luxury, normalcy.

"Talk to me, Lily," said Bonnie insistently, pulling me out of my reverie, "What brings you to Atlantic City?"

"I'm here to win."

"We're all here for that," she said.

"I need money to live."

"You're counting on winning?" she said, incredulously. "You barely know the rules of the game!"

"I don't know the rules about anything, Bonnie. I'm here because an incredible thing happened."

"Yeah?"

"A few weeks ago, I was in the Bahamas on New Year's Eve. It was after midnight. I'd had a lot of champagne, and went to a five-dollar blackjack table. I had never played for real money. The man beside me was betting heavily and losing. Just after I sat down, the cards got very hot. We began to win. He helped me play and pressed me into betting big -- bigger than I ever dreamed of betting. We covered every spot on the table and the streak just got hotter. We couldn't lose. I won twenty-thousand dollars that night."

"What luck!"

"I would never have bet that high and taken those chances under normal circumstances. But the champagne, the excitement of New Year's Eve, the beginning of a new decade, 1980, the lucky streak all catapulted me into the stratosphere. I've come here to ride that streak."

"You expect to make a living from gambling?"

"For a while."

"I've known a lot of guys who gamble. Some of them claim to make good money, but I've never known a woman to make a living from casino gambling. You've got to be desperate, Lily."

"Yes," I said, signaling for the waitress. We ordered another round of drinks.

"Those guys who grind it out," Bonnie said, "they aren't looking to make a big score. They don't take real chances."

"I don't have time to grind it out."

"You'd have an edge if you counted cards, at least some gamblers say that. I don't believe it."

"I couldn't ever manage that," I said. "It's much too difficult."

"Can't you raise money any other way?"

"No."

"That's tough, Lily. How long have you been married?"

"Almost sixteen years."

"What do you have of your own?"

"Nothing."

"Come on, Lily, don't tell me you didn't sock something away in all those rich years."

"It's true, Bonnie. I always believed I would be taken care of."

"Yeah, like the guy on New Year's Eve who helped you win. Like me tonight."

"Those were the conditions of my marriage, Bonnie. Paul controlled both the money and me. I was his baby, one of the kids. He lavished me with gifts. But the money was never mine, not half of it, not a quarter of it, nothing in my name, ever. It was his to give me -- and he was extremely generous."

"When he didn't give me what I wanted, I used the usual weapons: slyness, cajoling, sex, deference. I figured I could catch more flies with honey."

"Didn't you ever work?"

"We were married while I was still in school and I had three children in rapid succession. My job was wife and mother. It started out simply. We had no money and then Paul made a fortune. I became a caretaker and hostess. There was never any question of working."

"I understand now," she said. "You never had to take care of yourself. I learned how to do that very early in life and I never forget it. Sid and I have been married for nine years. He's as good a husband as you'll find: faithful, generous and loving. But I always remember one thing -- when I met him he was married to someone else."

"You're starting from scratch, Lily, and you'll have to learn fast. The casino's a place where you'll grow up quickly -- or not. If you do manage to win money, put it away for a rainy day."

Bonnie glanced at her considerable number of diamonds with a banker's eye.

"Solid platinum," she said, showing me her watch. "Twenty carats, blue-white diamonds, tripled in value in six months. A gift from Sid, like this diamond pin. She stroked her lapel, picking out the glittering stones with the sharp point of her fingernail.

"There's lots of ways of getting what you want in this world, Lily, and I don't think you've got a clue to any of them. Come and have dinner with me and I'll show you the ropes. You'll meet Sid, and besides, if you're with me, I'll have no trouble going back to the casino after dinner. And there's someone else I'd like you to meet."

"Who?"

"You'll see." She turned to me then, blue eyeliner in hand. "Do you have anybody else, a guy?"

"What do you mean?"

"You know, Lily, a lover."

"I can't answer that, Bonnie."

"Hey, your husband -- that's heavy stuff. We don't need to go into it. But lovers -- they're fair game, less real, more exciting. Don't worry, I'll keep it under my hat."

I quickly finished my drink. "Well, there was someone. I ended the affair about six months ago. He's one of those men who never really belong to any one woman."

"You mean he's a rat."

"Yes. I was addicted to him."

"Rats are like that -- they've got a smell you can't forget and you keep looking for it everywhere. One thing those guys do know, though, is how to give a girl a good time. In a sense, you were lucky. A real rat is hard to find."

"Too many complications," I said.

"Losses and gains, right? You get a little peace of mind back when it's over. You can get a good night's sleep, finally. It's like a rest cure, good for the nerves, but you don't feel so peppy."

"Right."

"The guy you had an affair with, does he have money?" She applied a smooth layer of lip-gloss.

"Yes."

"Well, if you're so hard up, why not ask him for a loan or something?"

"That's not my style."

"Hey babe, you've got to start using your head, and just maybe that means putting that fabulous face and figure to work for you. You're a great-looking broad. A little marketing wouldn't hurt."

Taking a last sip of my drink, I rose from the table, smiling. Bonnie was a marvelous tonic. She brightened my spirits and I happily accepted her dinner invitation. We went to the bathroom, where I washed my face and repaired the ravages of the day.

We walked arm-in-arm through the crowds, past a circular bar overflowing with revelers, past a female rock group called the G Strings and wearing little else, who were beating out the pulse of another Saturday night, past pale, local hookers, awkward and new to the trade, who smiled encouragingly while they tapped feet to the music; they hadn't yet acquired the veteran's stance of boredom.

The casino was alive with the carnival atmosphere of a big night in a small town and the scent of Saturday night sexuality was rampant. The women wore tight revealing clothes, heavy make-up and hair piled high in glossy tiaras that suggested the symbolic ornamentation of a tribal totem. They clutched their men fiercely, marking them as taken to all the lion-manned, nubile young girls eager to establish their own territorial imperative.

The men were as laden with jewels as the women. The older ones were more ornately adorned, as befitted rank and age. Medallions were encrusted with larger stones, and watches were laced with diamonds. Everyone was glossed and burnished with ointments and the air was redolent of the scent of a million cans of hair spray. Suddenly, I was happy to be in this noisy preposterous place, this garish gallery of limbo stuck out in the back end of the South Jersey swamps. I laughed aloud with pleasure.

"Boy, am I glad to finally see a smile on your face," said Bonnie. "When I sat down beside you at that table you looked as if you'd lost everything."

Bonnie was right. I had lost that safe clear space that I once believed was mine. The realm of the cherished wife, reliable mother, and adored mistress was gone. It had vanished. I was now, for the first time in my life, nobody's darling.

I had been brutally cast out of my world, forced to embark upon a relationship with the only person who could save me. I was thrust utterly upon the good graces of a perfect stranger. Myself.

CHAPTER TWO

The Golden Harp restaurant was Atlantic City deluxe: candlelight, tuxedoed waiters and Impressionistic murals depicting nymphs and satyrs frolicking in the Arcadia of South Jersey. The maitre d' bowed to Bonnie and escorted us to a secluded corner table where two men in their early sixties were having brandy, coffee and cigars. They rose as we approached.

Sid Fisher, dressed in a business suit, had an air of indulged affluence reflected in the clear pink of his baby skin. Jake Berman, silver-haired and tanned with translucent blue eyes, which lent his face a cast of indifference. He wore jeans, denim shirt and cowboy boots, a replica of my outfit.

"Bonnie found you a double, Jake," Sid said.

"Just what I've always wanted -- a twin!" said Jake.

"Jake's a real cowboy, he rode his horse to the airport in Vegas this morning. What's your excuse Lily?" asked Sid, smiling.

"Lily looks dynamite in jeans. That's good enough reason to wear them," Jake said, then turned to Bonnie. "If I'd known that you'd bring back a beauty, I'd have paged you hours ago."

My face grew hot.

"You're blushing," Jake said. "I didn't know that women still blushed -- it's lovely."

"I met Lily at a blackjack table tonight," Bonnie said. "We won together, probably because we were without our husbands. Since she's down here on her own, I invited her to join us for dinner."

Jack signaled to the maitre d' who responded by bringing caviar and champagne.

"Doesn't your husband gamble?" Jake asked.

"Not in casinos."

"I'm happy you left the table winning, Bonnie," Sid said, "instead of giving it all back then and there. Your losing may be good for business, but it's bad for my morale." He softened his chastisement with a hug. "Are you a blackjack fanatic too, Lily?"

"I've really just begun to play," I said. "This is my first time in Atlantic City."

"Lily hit a lucky streak in the Bahamas recently and she decided to come down here and ride it out," Bonnie said.

"Beginner's luck -- that's the best kind, rubs off on everyone around the winner," said Jake.

"That's it!" exclaimed Bonnie. "I should've known! I sat down beside Lily, played one unit for a while, and then all of a sudden, on a whim, I bet everything and got a blackjack. We're a winning team, Lily. You're my lucky charm. We've got to play together after dinner."

"Gamblers are notoriously superstitious," Sid said.

"The world loves a winner," Jake said.

"And a lover," Sid said.

"Being lucky is like falling in love," Bonnie said.

"Shakespeare compared falling in love to catching the plague," I said. "Perhaps the sense of imminent disaster is part of the attraction -- like the risk in gambling. Look at Tristan and Isolde, Romeo and Juliet, Heloise and Abelard, Adam and Eve, for that matter -- they knew the terror of that leap, that *fall* into love. It's the ultimate risk and the ultimate luck."

"What a romantic you are, Lily. The next thing you'll be telling me is that you're here to beat the house," Jake said.

"That's right," I said.

"I won't ruin your illusions then," Jake said. "I know that winning means more than just making money. Everyone wants to feel fortunate. That's why the search gets so desperate in a casino."

"If you keep coming back you've got to lose even if you're a card counter. It's the human element that's dangerous and then the game becomes a costly amusement," said Sid.

"No lecturing at dinner," Bonnie said.

"You'll give the business a bad name, Sid," Jake said. "Most pleasures are expensive, one way or another. I try to keep mine to a minimum to avoid excitement as I get older."

"Jake collects paintings," Bonnie said.

"Hardly a Spartan pleasure," I said.

"There's more gambling outside casinos than in them," Bonnie said. "Sid's heavily into the stock market, has been for years and continues to play and win, at least that's what I hear. And Jake takes in profits from paintings. Both of you guys are horse traders in a very big way."

"The point of buying and selling pictures is not to make money but to improve the collection," Sid said, "and the stock market's business."

"Yeah, yeah," said Bonnie dryly.

The conversation was halted by the arrival of a menu bound with the care given a first folio. Jake banished it with a wave of his hand before we could look at it.

"Order anything," he said.

The caviar had more than appeased my hunger, but Jake, ignored my demurral and ordered a rare steak for me. I was amused at his presumption.

"Jake's our leader," Bonnie said. "He runs the show and he's almost never wrong, he makes everybody happy and anticipates wishes before you're aware of them yourself. Isn't that right, Sid?"

"You betcha baby, Jake's the supreme commander," Sid said.

"Last month Sid hadn't been feeling well," said Bonnie. "We were on the East coast, due to fly to Washington on the company jet for a business meeting, but instead Jake arranged to have us flown to Tahiti. Imagine! We got off the plane expecting rain and found paradise."

"You see, Lily, I promise no less than heaven," Jake said, smiling at me.

"When we arrived at the villa," Bonnie continued, "everything was set up for us, down to the smallest detail. Servants, exotic foods, flowers, clothes, toilet articles, perfumes, bathing suits, gifts, even Sid's favorite brandy. It was a dream come true. We were magically transported away from everything."

"It sounds perfect," I said, barely able to envision the pleasures that Bonnie described, although luxury had been the essential quality of my own life for many years.

The champagne hit suddenly, carrying me to the top, where everything was soft and easy. I'd been away from home for barely six hours, but it felt like years.

The intoxicating air of blatant sexuality, which I'd sensed in the casino, was now, in this atmosphere of sham elegance and real affluence, transformed into a subtler essence. The tensions of gambling and sexuality created a mood of excitement that silently met and spurred Jake's interest. My blush was not the result of modesty. It was, rather, a banked fire prepared to flare at any spark.

"We're leaving early tomorrow for the Bahamas on company business and then back to New York for the auction, right Jake?" Bonnie said.

"Of course."

"Are we still on for Antibes for next weekend?"

"No, it's off." He turned to me. "I've had a villa in Cap Ferrat for years and I was recently offered adjacent acreage. We were using the contract signing for an excuse for a French food binge, but it's been postponed."

"The adjacent land is the size of Monaco," said Bonnie.

I listened as the moneyed talk and worldly gossip swirled around me, about race horses, private islands, lavish parties,

Midas touches, yachting trips, St. Moritz, collections, charity balls, political movers and the overwhelmingly public life of the wealthy and powerful.

A handsome young man with an Italian accent joined us. Marco D'Amato worked for Jake and he brought news that changed Jake's mood at once. The three men spoke together, Jake's voice becoming clipped and cold as he fired off instructions. Bonnie and I sipped our champagne in silence. Gradually the shift in focus altered my mood and the luxury of the scene began once more to seem illusory.

As the champagne began its downward slide, I felt my mood swinging. I didn't belong here, dining with strangers, receiving the amorous attentions of a man whom I'd just met. Having lost my moorings, I was in danger of becoming a drifter, living on the edge of other people's lives. The fear and fatigue that had been masked by gambling's adrenaline, the wine and the effervescence of sexual excitement stopped me as if a brake had been pressed.

"Forgive me," I said, rising. "I'm dizzy and I think I'd better go back to my room."

Bonnie was offering to accompany me when Jake, in a rapid motion, stood up and took my arm.

"It's stifling in here, let's get some air."

He didn't wait for my reply, but steered me out of the restaurant through the lobby and out into the street. Snow had begun to fall and the air was soft and mild. Jake put his jacket on my shoulders and we walked out onto the boardwalk and took shelter under a canopied storefront.

The lamplight shone dimly on abandoned play land rides, creating mythic monoliths, relics of an ancient Atlantis. Charmed by the calm beauty of the night, we were silent, watching the snowflakes spiral into the sky.

"What happened in the restaurant, Lily?" he asked.

"Smoke, drink and excitement -- it was all too much. I was getting very high."

"Don't panic," he said. "You'll be fine soon. We'll stay here till you're under control. You didn't drink enough champagne to get drunk."

"I just feel very strange."

"Gambling pulls out all the stops, makes you crazy."

"I've only been in one small casino in the Caribbean. This place is overwhelming."

"The power of greed is fantastic. Easy money brings out all the savage instincts, very heady stuff."

"It makes you feel high, like a drug."

"You're here alone, that's a big difference, and you're used to the regularity of family life. A casino's a madhouse."

"It actually translates as madhouse in Italian, and as a brothel," I said.

"Yes. In a casino, you've got the collective whorish madness of humanity."

"Aren't you bad-mouthing the hand that feeds you?"

"I'm not on company time now. Not when I'm with you. Besides, I don't look at you as a major customer or high roller. But how come you're here alone, without your husband?"

"It's a very long story."

"I hope we'll find time for that long story," he said, turning to gaze into my face. "But, Lily," he said, "Leave as soon as you can. The atmosphere is poison and if you breathe it too long, you'll catch the illness. People come here for all kinds of reasons -- excitement, titillation, escape, sex, money, drugs, to shake off boredom and pain. Let loose in a casino, even the sanest person goes crazy."

"Well, I'm really here because I need the money," I said.

"Seriously?"

"Yes."

"I'd have guessed you were here for a little excitement or escape."

"I'm not adverse to those either."

"But you're here to win money to live?"

"Yes."

"Oh, God, another believer!"

"Sometimes you've got to take what life offers. I never imagined it would come to this." I began to cry. "Look at me, I'm drunk and hysterical with an absolute stranger."

"I'm not such a stranger. Cry it out, you'll feel better. Talking helps." He gave me his handkerchief and I cried quietly for a few minutes.

"Forgive me, Jake, I'm ruining your evening."

"I'm sorry your life's so hard now, Lily, but I'm glad to be here with you."

"I feel like such a fool."

"If you hadn't come along, it would've been the same boring routine -- dinner, business, bed. It's extraordinary for me to leave the rut, to be somewhere other than where I'm supposed to be. How often do you think I get to watch a snowstorm on the boardwalk in Atlantic City with a captivating woman? You make me feel like a kid, Lily."

"That's because I've behaved like a child."

"You're in some kind of real trouble, Lily. I don't know the details, but it's serious and cause for tears. You're human and scared. But for me, I'm pleased I met you. I thought that there weren't any woman like you around anymore, that they'd broken the mold."

"Which mold is that?" I asked.

"You're naive, guileless," he said. "The qualities of women of my generation."

"The qualities of a child."

"I spend the whole of my life with people who never tell the truth about anything. Every con has another one behind it, every scam is tripled, ambiguity is everything. It's a delight to be with a woman who's open, not challenging, attacking or playing out some vicious game. Women aren't like that anymore."

"Like what?" I asked.

"Simple. Even the chorus girls in Vegas are liberated."

"Women were never simple, Jake. They just pretended. Naiveté in a girl of eighteen is okay, but in a woman of almost thirty-six, it's grotesque and a great handicap. Innocence is only for the very young."

"It's a charming quality at any age, Lily, and it's especially rare among the inhabitants of Los Angeles and Las Vegas, the two cities I've lived in for the past twenty years. No, Lily, you're the last of a dying breed, a soft, sweet woman, one to be indulged and protected."

"If I were as guileless as you imagine, I wouldn't be on the boardwalk at night with a man I've known scarcely an hour."

"Time is accelerated in a casino. An hour is equivalent to a month, a day to a year, and although you feel reckless, you're an atavism, Lily, a variety of a near extinct species, the old fashioned girl of my long, lost youth. I recognized you instinctively. I grew up with girls like you, my first wife was like you, married young, never went out in the world. She never had to prove herself."

"That was true for me, until now," I said. "But I've paid heavily for being indulged and protected. I have to grow up fast, take charge and be boss."

"Old-fashioned girls can be boss. If that's what you want."

An icy blast of wind came off the ocean, forcing us to return to the hotel. When we entered the lobby, Jake jotted a number on the back of a card and handed it to me.

"I'd like very much to see you, Lily. Call me soon. It's my private number at home. I can always be reached. If I didn't have to work now and fly out early in the morning, I'd love to spend more time with you. Let's get back and finish your dinner."

"I'm not hungry," I said. "You're not the only one who has to work tonight. I've got to clear my head and get back to the casino."

"You've chosen a strange way to declare your independence."

"I didn't choose it. It happened."

"Be careful, Lily," Jake said, taking his jacket from my shoulders, "the tables will swallow you up whole and you'll never see the blood. You'll never know they've killed you, until it's too late."

In the restaurant over coffee, Sid and Jake continued to talk business. Marco had left and after a few minutes Bonnie said, "Let's go to my suite. I'd like to freshen up."

The moment we closed the door Bonnie hugged me with a whoop of laughter. "You've been playing the wrong tables Lily. You just hit the multimillion-dollar jackpot!"

"What do you mean, Bonnie?"

"Jake, he's very interested in you. I've never seen him so attentive to a woman. Did he ask to see you again?"

"He gave me his home phone and asked me to call him soon."

"And?"

"I can't call him."

"Why not?"

"What's the point, Bonnie? I broke off an affair with someone I was crazy about because it was complicated and nerve-wracking. I made the mistake of getting involved while I was married. It's hell for everyone. I just couldn't resist it then, but now I've got to keep my priorities clear. Everything rests on me. Besides, Bonnie, I don't know if I'm even interested in Jake."

"Do you know *who* Jake Berman is?"

"A business associate of Sid's."

Bonnie took a deep breath and when she spoke, it was in hushed tones, enunciating each word clearly. "Jake Berman is one of the richest and most powerful men in the country. He controls vast conglomerates, like the one that owns this hotel. He's into everything: ballistics, newspapers, and real estate. And if that isn't enough, he's good-looking and an art collector of international repute. But best of all, Lily, he's unattached, which makes him the eighth and ninth wonders of the world. Sid's known him for years. He's respected, generous, and he's been wonderful to us." Bonnie paused to see the effects of her speech. "Well, are you interested now, Lily?"

"I don't know what you're really asking me, Bonnie."

"In your position a guy like Jake could be the answer for you, in every way. He's part of your lucky streak, the pot of gold at the end of the rainbow. You can never tell where something like this might lead. I'm sure he'd want to marry again, if the right woman came along."

"I'm already married to one supreme commander, Bonnie. But don't fool me or yourself. If Jake's interested in me, it's for the thing that all men want, an affair with no headaches before, during or after. I'm flattered by his attentions, but I've already had the last of the red-hot lovers."

"I'm not talking sex, Lily, I'm talking megabucks." She smoothed the lapel of her jacket and touched her diamond rose. "I'm talking real power."

"You're describing payment for sexual favors, Bonnie, and there's only one name for that, no matter how expensive the favor or how charming the transaction."

"Jake's a great guy with women," she said defensively. "He's usually got one heavy number at a time, but at this moment, lucky you, he doesn't have anyone steady."

"What happened to his wife?"

"She was killed in a car crash about thirteen years ago. They were childhood sweethearts, just mad about each other, didn't need anyone else, really. He was devastated. The kids were grown by then and a couple of years later he married some socialite type from San Francisco. That was short and not so sweet. She took him for a bundle and since then Jake's been fair game for the ladies.

"I've seen him with all kinds of women over the years. He's always kind and polite but he seemed bowled over by you. I've never seen him so attracted or involved so quickly. It was like he knew you already -- like love at first sight."

"You've got a great imagination, Bonnie."

"Do you like him at all, Lily?"

"He's kind and he has extraordinary eyes."

"That's a beginning, anyway," she said, laughing.

Bonnie left the room and returned in a few minutes with a black, velvet jewelry case. "You sure lucked out on all counts tonight, Lily. I've got a real treat for you. This stuff is amazing." She sat down on the sofa beside me.

"I'm exhausted, Bonnie," I said.

"This is just the thing to get you up and roaring. A quick blast of toot and you'll be righter than rain. This is the best blow in the world. I crushed it myself."

"Cocaine?" I asked.

"Oh yes," she said. "Don't tell me you've never tried it."

"No."

"Well, there's a first time for everything. You'll love it."

She poured the white powder on a large hand mirror, forming two long lines with a thin, silver knife. She handed me a tightly rolled hundred-dollar bill.

"Hold one nostril tight while you sniff up high and strong with the other," she said. "Then reverse."

I didn't pause. Bending over the mirror, I looked into the kohl-rimmed black eyes, magnified between the lines of cocaine. The lashes were thickly coated with mascara, like the antennae of some still, wary insect. The evil eye was my own. I followed Bonnie's instructions and after a minute, I was more alert, but hardly euphoric. She wasted no words now, but poured double the amount of cocaine on the mirror and cut it into four thick lines, two for each nostril. In rapid succession, I snorted the lines of white powder.

The second blast was instantaneous, sharp and exquisite. From the far reaches of helpless anguish, I was rocketed into an orbit of bright perception. It was the promise of Mephistopheles, the magic of Jekyll and the power of Proteus. In the space of a second, I was reborn. All possibilities were given back to me, time was made malleable, and dross had become gold. I had only to find the winning table.

CHAPTER THREE

seized the moment and glided buoyantly into the crush and clamor of the casino at midnight. The open anchor seat at a hundred-dollar minimum table, matched with my mood of expansive invincibility, overwhelmed caution and I ordered a marker for a thousand dollars. Bonnie disappeared.

Although the patrons in this expensive enclave were treated with greater deference than at the lower-limit tables, they seemed in no way different or more affluent. They were, however, a good deal grimmer.

A very old lady sat opposite me wearing a red sequined dress. She had platinum hair, a ton of make-up and a cane clutched in her gnarled hand. Years before, I would have dismissed her as hopelessly vulgar, dressed in clothes suitable to a woman half her age, but I knew better now. Those wildly inappropriate tresses and red sequins were the woman's battle standard, an embodiment of her courage.

Seated beside this old warrior was a young man impersonating a rock star. He had long, curly hair and wore white leather. Assuming a bored, disdainful air, he shifted his chips constantly from one hand to the other. When his eyes weren't on the cards, he stared into the distance, unwilling to be associated with the other players.

The third member of the table was lean and boyish with regular, undistinguished features and straight brown hair falling across his forehead. He wore a tweed jacket reinforced with suede at the elbows and a turtleneck sweater. These small distinguishing traits and his utter stillness marked him as the first Wasp I had seen in a casino exploding with ethnics.

He glanced at me surreptitiously several times. I sensed that little eluded him, that his mind was as nimble as his eye. He chain-smoked, using an ancient Zippo lighter, and when he ordered a double bourbon, he spoke in a cultivated mid-Atlantic tone.

I looked at my companions of the night and wondered at the voyages of their hearts and minds, each charting a different course, yet bound and bonded by this table, all of us supplicants to the same gods. Once more the world seemed full of surprise, wonder and delight. It didn't matter that I was riding a cocaine high. I flew along, feeling rich and full, vision intensified, spurred by the leaps and twists of imagination and the excitement of the cards. Ideas and images flashed through my mind with breathtaking brilliance. My body felt light and I could feel the pull of skin, tight and perfect over my bones.

At last the shoe ended, the cards were shuffled and we were ready. Each shoe was a chance for a new beginning. I looked at the ten black one hundred dollar chips and tried not to think about how quickly they could disappear into the dealer's coffers. The old lady, as if answering my thoughts, said in a quavering voice, "Thank heaven that shoe's over. A new shoe, that's what we need, to begin again, eh fellas?"

She laughed, inviting the others to respond and received a grudging nod from the rock star and a sedate "Always" from the Wasp. Apparently the last shoe had been a disaster.

Just before the first hand was dealt, three jolly conventioneers joined the table. My momentary fear dispelled, I felt luck rushing toward me and when I was dealt a blackjack on the first round, it seemed as inevitable as sunrise.

The others were betting heavily, more than a thousand a hand and although the cocaine and the high stakes had sharpened the excitement, I didn't double my bet, but continued playing one unit of a hundred dollars. My luck held and at the end of the shoe, I was ahead a thousand dollars.

It had been a lucky shoe for everyone and the table was in high spirits, smiling, chatting and ordering drinks. There is no greater spur to conviviality than winning. Even the rock star, from his Olympian heights of egotism, deigned to answer the old lady's questions concerning the play. The Wasp and I were silent. He played extremely well, with utter concentration and once the shoe had begun, his eyes never left the cards. He seemed to be betting less and winning more consistently than the others. I watched his play closely and realized that he was counting cards.

He was careful not to call attention to himself by increasing his bets dramatically, since card counters were banned from the casinos. Unable to resist adding his edge to my luck, I began to follow his betting patterns.

The effects of the cocaine had vanished when suddenly I felt as if I'd fallen into a well. I became dizzy and weak. The cards, however, were still running hot, and like an overtired child, I didn't want to stop. I placed the chips in my bag, reserved my seat, and walked shakily to the ladies room.

I splashed cold water on my face, stretched and took deep breaths, but couldn't revive myself. And then I remembered the cocaine that Bonnie had given me before we left the suite.

The bathroom was almost deserted. Entering a cubicle at the far end, I sat down on the covered toilet and took out the jar of white powder, repeating Bonnie's motions, pouring the drug onto my compact mirror, arranging the rails with the flat end of a match-book cover and, using my handbag as a bolster, balancing everything on my knees. I was amazed at the agility of my hands and fingers in that tight space.

Rolling a dollar bill, I sniffed up the cocaine greedily, quickly rationalizing that two hits do not an addict make. When I envisioned all that faced me at home, I was tempted to sniff myself into another galaxy.

The vial of cocaine slipped to the floor, and as I bent to retrieve it, I was transported to another time, on a summer evening long ago, bending then, to pluck a white rose for my hair. And from the cocaine snorter crouching in a toilet, I became again what I had once been: loved, protected, rich and privileged.

Strolling on the deep green lawns of our summer house in East Hampton, I was hostess at a benefit. The intellectual and social elite who were expiating their guilt by contributing large sums of money in the absurdly convivial surroundings of a palatial beach front estate. There were glamorous guests strolling about the cantilevered Roman pool, rare shrubs, maids serving canapés and butlers fixing drinks.

The destiny of the woman with the white rose in her hair had wound down to this image now, crouching in a bathroom cubicle at a casino in the early hours of a Sunday morning, alone, snorting cocaine. What transfigurations, I wondered, unimaginable now, would rise to astonish me in the future?

The blast hit and the melancholic vision was transformed into an intimation of delight. I laughed aloud with sudden giddy pleasure, opened the door and ran into Bonnie.

"You seem to be having the time of your life," she said.

"I'm winning," I said, "and I can see by your face that "you must've won a fortune, Bonnie."

Easy and smiling, Bonnie looked like one of life's winners, as fresh and elegant as I'd first seen her hours before. "I won a fortune," she said, "but stayed too long. I was ahead forty thousand and wound up losing fifty thousand."

"How awful," I said.

"You win some, you lose some," she said, shrugging her shoulders.

Bonnie was neither upset nor discouraged. Instead, she looked remarkably satisfied. Apparently she'd gotten what she wanted and in some cosmic bookkeeping, her figures tallied. We exchanged addresses and phone numbers, promising to keep in touch. She came to Atlantic City often. We were outside the ladies' room when she asked me if I'd ever been to Vegas.

"No, never," I said.

She smiled broadly. "Then I've got a great idea. I'll arrange for you to come on a junket. It'll be terrific -- everything on the house, except for gambling money, and you'll go in style. Gambling's the real thing in Vegas -- it's more fun than anywhere else, fast and wild, heavy rollers and lots of flesh and flash. You can keep those old European Baden-Badens and bury them; everything's so slow. I almost fell asleep at the tables in Monte Carlo. You'll see Jake's ranch and art collection. And of course, it'll be good for me to have you around. Besides, Lily, you're my kind of lady, I wouldn't invite you otherwise. "

Riding the cocaine, I accepted her invitation at once. I loved the idea, and I was beginning to understand Bonnie's addiction to blackjack. It made me like her all the better.

Bubbling with good cheer, I winged my way back to the baccarat area and slid smoothly into my chair at third base. In place of my former quiet enjoyment, I was now beaming and expansive, anxious and impelled to speak.

"You look like the cat who swallowed the canary," a chubby conventioneer said.

"Yeah, we missed you honey," another party boy said. "You're one helluva anchor lady. We've been losing ever since you left."

The Wasp rose, preparing to leave. I felt a pang of disappointment until I heard him ask the dealer to reserve his seat. He looked over at me.

"Watch yourself till I get back," he said in a low voice.

He had noticed me following his betting patterns. When he returned we didn't glance at or speak to one another. I'd been foolish to follow his lead so blindly. One counter at the table was more than enough.

Feeling loose and lucky I began to raise my bets while engaging the dealer, the pit bosses and the other players in meaningless chatter. I simply couldn't stop talking. The merriest of the party boys, an overgrown sophomoric type with tie askew and rumpled hair, addressed me.

"Hey, sleeping beauty, what happened to you? You're quiet as a mouse, go to the ladies' room and presto, you're a talker?"

I didn't reply.

"We've got a party going on in our suite for two days now. Food, drink, music, the works. How's about coming up and helping us celebrate our winnings? And, boy, have we won a bundle."

"No thank you," I said. They pressed me to join them until it became an irritating game. Apparently my volubility had given them the cue to come on to me. The Wasp returned to the table, and in a moment of mischievous inspiration, I looked at him.

"I'm already spoken for -- I'm with that gentleman," I said, nodding my head toward the Wasp.

"Well, lady, you should've said so first off and wouldn't have bothered you," said the chubby man.

"Gee, we didn't know she was with you. No offense meant," another man said. "She is with you, right?"

All eyes were on the Wasp. I held my breath and swallowed my giggles. He looked up and said,

"Yes, she's with me and has been, all the way."

The tension broke. I was delighted with my new mentor. He'd shown both humor and graciousness in dealing with the silly situation that I'd thrust upon him. Of course, it would have been embarrassing if a wife or girl friend arrived now to claim him, but he had about him the stillness of the solitary and I sensed that he was alone.

The conventioneers left soon after, followed by the old lady and the rock star. It was strange how quickly the foreign became familiar, almost intimate, in a casino. Having grown accustomed to a presence, I felt a fleeting sadness at each parting.

Glancing at my fellow conspirator, certain that he was counting, I again began to follow his lead. Only hours before I would have shuddered at the idea of betting five hundred dollars on a single card, but I was now betting that amount with equanimity, rationalizing that counting cards increased my edge and that I was winning.

Gambling odds have been computerized. One can win under certain conditions, if one adheres to a structure as formal as a Mass and achieves a state of Grace, whose worldly equivalent is luck. I was now in that gambler's state of Grace, using a perfect basic strategy, counting cards, and in possession of that most mercurial of all elements, pure luck.

The cards floated in gently, as if in a preordained sequence; aces, kings, queens and tens. Each hand had a magic beat, echoing the throb of my heart. Time was encapsulated in the narrow world of hand signals, the click and movement of chips and my covert glances at the Wasp. Although I used his expertise, there was no perceptible communication between us; only the shared danger of high-stakes, gambling and the subtler thrill of an invisible, electric wire of sexual attraction.

Superstitious, I dared not count my chips. I seemed to have been playing for an eternity, but it might have been no more than ten minutes. There are no clocks in casinos. In the passionate pursuit of escape, time is obliterated. My cocaine high had vanished and I was playing on the last shreds of an attenuated nervous energy.

With a motion of rapid, graceful economy, the Wasp stood up, flipped a pile of chips into his pocket and walked over to me.

"You've won enough for tonight. Time to go."

His advice seemed apt and I rose to leave. The dealer changed my black chips into fourteen five hundred dollar chips. I'd won roughly seven thousand dollars. Leaving a hundred-dollar tip for the dealer, I dutifully followed my leader out of the baccarat area. We walked in silence to the cashier. When we reached the window, I held out my hand.

"Lily Jarman," I said.

"Nick Van Pelt," he said, shaking my hand. "Let's get a drink at the bar, it's been a very thirsty night."

We cashed in our chips. I ordered a drink and went to place my money in the safety deposit box. Looking at the small mountain of hundred-dollar bills, I waited for a sense of elation but felt nothing. I was drained of all emotion, even that of victory.

Nick waited for me at the bar, a lone figure outlined against the neon-lit mirrors. We drank stingers, strong and sweet. Too depleted to talk, we smoked in companionable silence, slowly coming down from the vertiginous high of the cards.

"The double counting caper is like a high-wire act with no net. Not to be repeated," he said.

We laughed, releasing the tensions of gambling and acknowledging the strong sexual aura that was implicit in our being together in this place, at this hour.

"Where did you learn to count cards?" I asked.

"I've read a great deal and attended seminars on counting in Oregon and Nevada."

"You were kind to let me borrow your expertise," I said.

"I didn't have much choice."

"You could've changed tables."

"The cards got very hot after you sat down. One can wait a very long time for a run like that. But it was dangerous for both of us to be counting. I saw the pit bosses staring. We could've been banned from playing."

"Is that the only reason you stayed?" I asked.

"Well, in part, I stayed because it *was* dangerous," he said. "It added an element of risk to an explosive situation. Besides, I loved watching your opulent dissipation."

"Was it worth the risk?" I asked.

"Yes, on both counts," he said, "and you did bring a lucky streak."

"I won a great deal, thanks to you," I said.

"You had the cards, Lily, you couldn't do anything wrong."

"How often do you get down to Atlantic City?" I asked.

"I've been coming here ever since the first hotel opened two years ago, in seventy-eight. I manage to get down every couple of months. It's one of the great all-time highs. And addictions."

"Winning feels like flying," I said.

Another round of drinks appeared. We had begun to celebrate our luck and each other, dutifully supplying small bits of biography for the sake of some long out-moded form of courtesy. Nick was twenty-eight, younger than I'd thought, an authentic Eastern Wasp -- St. Paul's and Harvard. He had remained in Cambridge after graduating, using an inheritance to publish a literary magazine. An instructor in American literature at a small college, he was writing a novel. Nicholas Snow Van Pelt, poor little rich boy, orphaned, unmarried, literary.

We drank the last offerings of the night. The phosphorescent lights of the bar cast a luminous light on our faces, like swimmers under water. When we touched hands, as if at a signal, I knew that I'd go to bed with him.

I thought of Jake then, saw the image of his worldly weathered face and it seemed that I'd known him, not hours ago, but in another life, and that I was now living in a later incarnation, conscious of the urgency and breathless speed with which I was devouring time.

"You look strange and beautiful in this light, like a statue," Nick said, breaking into my musing.

"'Je suis belle, o mortels! comme un reve de pierre,'" I quoted.

"Baudelaire, the poet of the night. How appropriate, Lily."

"If I've begun to quote poetry..."

"Then clearly it's time to leave," he said, kissing me lightly on the mouth.

Suddenly my bravado faded.

"Don't tell me, let me guess," he said. "You've never done this before."

"That would be untrue."

"Isn't that what you were about to say?" he asked.

"I want to tell you that I'm married, have three daughters and have never had a real one-night stand. What began as an adventure sixteen years ago became a marriage."

"You don't have to explain. It doesn't matter, Lily. I can sense things. It's really a question of faith."

"To faith," I said, raising my glass in a toast.

"To more than an adventure -- to us," said Nick.

When we opened the door to my room, thin slants of daylight were filtering through the drapes. I closed them tightly.

"Shall I order champagne to celebrate our winnings properly?" he asked.

"Yes," I said, and lay down on the bed.

Nick called room service, then pulled off my boots and lay down on the adjacent bed. "Has there been anyone in your life since you've been married?" he asked.

"You are curious in spite of yourself, Nick."

"One can be curious without it mattering."

"I'm not going to enlighten you. Just think of me as a woman of mystery."

"There's nothing more mysterious than a beautiful woman gambling alone in a casino," he said.

The food and drink were brought by a waiter who had the perfect air for delivering celebratory suppers at six in the morning.

"Winners," he assessed.

"Yes!" we replied together.

"In every way," Nick added.

The waiter opened the champagne with a flourish and exited, enjoining us, "Enjoy, kiddies, enjoy!"

We toasted and Nick lit a joint, passing it to me. We lay smoking grass and drinking champagne.

"You were on coke before, weren't you, Lily?"

"Was it obvious?"

"Only to an old snow nose like me," he said, moving to lie beside me. "I was thinking of making love to you all night as I watched you spending yourself so prodigally."

"And you preferred that I spend myself on you?"

"Yes," Nick said, kissing the back of my neck. "You struck me as marvelously excessive."

"I wish I could comply with your desires, but I can't move -- champagne, cocaine, brandy, grass, more champagne."

"You've just been a bad kid, Lily, not to worry. I'll revive you."

Nick turned down the covers, swooped me up and lay me down on the cool sheets. He took off my shirt and jeans, then went into the bathroom. I could hear the water running.

"Your bath is ready, Madame," he said.

I bathed quickly, wrapped myself in towels and fell back into the bed.

"You're such a good Mommy," I said. Like Janis Joplin sang -- 'get it while you can'.

I turned on my stomach and Nick gently massaged my neck and shoulders.

"How long have you been playing?" he asked.

"Since about seven this evening."

"Have you eaten anything substantial?" he asked.

"Chocolate bars and caviar."

"You certainly are excessive, Lily. What you need is food."

I watched him move around the room, lithe, graceful and young. He propped me up with pillows, tucked me under the covers and brought a plate of sandwiches.

"You're sweet," I said.

"I've got an ulterior motive," he leered in mock villainy.

"I'm afraid you're doomed to disappointment, I'm exhausted."

"Time for Van Pelt's last resort," he said, producing a heaping dish of chocolate ice cream topped with melting fudge which he spooned into my mouth.

"Ah, how clever of you," I said.

Nick kissed my mouth, all icy sweet with chocolate, with his lips, warm and champagne tart, and we laughed with the sheer play of it, until there was only the taste of lips and the evocative pressure of skin.

He undressed in a single, swift motion, threw back the covers and stood above me. Poised for pleasure, we held the moment, our eyes locked in a doubled beam, illuminating our nakedness and the deeper glow of desire.

Nick came into the bed and with a motion infinitely tender, lifted my hair and kissed the nape of my neck. His warm breath lingered on the secret skin, his kisses quickening pleasure as he moved his lips down my back.

We made love with an extravagantly slow voluptuousness, the self-eclipsed under the explosive radiations of erotic joy. At last I had arrived at the oblivion I had longed for, a sensuous abandon of skin and muscle, touch and caress, without history, without love, charged with the excitement of wild adventure.

And yet, somewhere deep in mindless exaltation, a pain sharp and keen as a dagger's thrust, a longing that grabs at the throat, a split-second agony of a remembered touch, and then, in a blinding instant, the reprieve, the act of God, the release.

Before sleep claimed me, my eyes opened and I looked into the face of the sleeping stranger within whose arms I lay.

CHAPTER FOUR

The ring of the telephone exploding into the room awakened me.

"Lily Jarman," a lilting West Indian voice demanded, "Nassau, Bahamas, calling. One moment please."

Waiting for the connection in a state of panic and disorientation, I was unable to decipher my surroundings. I was in a darkened, anonymous room, naked, lying next to an alien, sleeping figure whose arm lay flung across my body in a gesture of possession. My head throbbed, my throat burned and every bone and muscle felt as if it had been twisted for maximum pain.

I groped for a cigarette but could find none among the litter on the table near the bed. I lit a butt from an overflowing ashtray as a man's voice came on the line.

"Hello, Lily, this is Jake Berman. We got down about an hour ago and we're at poolside having lunch. Come down and join us. The weather's glorious and there are blackjack tables here too. I'll send the plane back up for you. How about it, Lily?"

Relieved that the call was not Paul or the children, I took a quaff of warm champagne and, in a voice thickened with smoke and sleep, declined the invitation. He asked me to call him soon and told me that he was very intrigued.

Reaching into my bag for aspirins, I was startled at the sound of another man's voice at my shoulder.

"Not your husband, I presume," said Nick.

"You presume correctly," I said.

"Who are you really, Lily Jarman?" he asked.

"What you're asking," I said huskily, still searching in my bag, "is what role will I play in your life."

"Okay?"

"I shall be your Madame Bovary," I said, draping a loosened sheet around me, walking into the bathroom and turning on the shower.

"I'll settle for that," he said, scurrying after me.

"Of course you'll settle for that, it's what drew you to me. That's what all writers live for, to "live" it, in order to have it inside, to tap it when it's needed, like money hidden in a Swiss account. You'll settle for that, indeed. It's what you want above anything."

Nick pulled off the sheet and held me against him, whispering into my ear provocatively, "The tables or the bed, Madame?"

"The tables, of course, and quickly."

The steaming water relaxed my muscles and by the time I emerged from the shower, I was greeted with the surprise of freshly brewed coffee and the comforting smell of toasted bread. Nick pulled out my chair and seated me with a flourish. After eating we took our coffee cups to the bed and lazed, legs intertwined. I was astonished at how quickly and simply I had fallen into this new intimacy.

Only a few years before, in the first shattering breach of marital fidelity, I had been torn apart by those conflicting passions, loyalty and desire. I had never imagined sex as a casual encounter, the simple proximity of a naked body, a bed and a locked room. It had always been symbolized for me by the idea of marriage or a fatal passion. I'd been an anachronism in an age of sexual freedom.

And now I knew with certainty that in place of Nick's pale, boyish face I could have just as easily been looking into Jake's shrewd, sun-darkened visage. It was difficult to know if I was realizing a gift for intimacy or developing a latent penchant for promiscuity. I sensed that my rapacious sexual stirrings were providing me with fuel, a tapping of the bed-rock, the mother-lode for hidden energy to keep me going.

"The last romantic is dead," I said, kissing Nick hard on the mouth.

"You really hadn't done this before," he said. "You've lost your illusions after last night. Are you sorry?"

"Of course not," I said, "but I'm surprised. One-night stands are meant to be demeaning, disappointing and sleazy, but it wasn't at all like that, last night or now."

"Not everything's difficult, or life and death either, Lily. Some things are lucky, easy and gratuitous. But if you're disillusioned, I'll assume that the mantle has fallen upon my shoulders and that now I'm the last romantic."

He embraced me passionately, kissing my face and neck.

"I think I'm going to fall in love with you, Lily."

"Oh Nick, I'm merely a bit of exotica for you." I stood up and began to dress.

"Nonsense, Lily," he said, turning to me and looking into my eyes. "You know, I sense that there's another man in the picture, besides your husband. Not the man on the phone this morning, someone else. In any case, my love is doomed to be unrequited." He did not look unhappy at the prospect.

"It will improve your writing," I said. "It's the perfect apprenticeship."

"And what shall I be for you, Lily, your gigolo?"

"Don't be silly, Wasps can't be gigolos. You'll be my tour guide, my card counter."

He grew serious. "We really can't do that anymore. It was a miracle that we weren't caught last night. The pit bosses were getting suspicious. And that doesn't do at all."

"Oh God, no," I said, frightened at the thought that I'd risked my only means of making money. I grew silent as the reality of my situation entered the soft luxury of our mid-day idyll. Tears unexpectedly stung my eyes and I turned away abruptly.

"What's wrong, Lily?" Nick asked. "When I mentioned being banned from playing, your face lost all color." He sat up suddenly, facing me. "This money is really important to you, isn't it, you really need this money?"

I nodded.

"Through the haze of booze last night, I knew that one element of the picture was missing," he said.

"It was strange for someone like you to be here alone. The pieces didn't fit. I assumed there were marital problems, that you were under a great strain, but I never suspected that you weren't what you appeared to be -- slumming, out for a romp, wallowing in a grand *nostalgie de la boue*. God, Lily, you even have a tan!"

And then he said, "It's all on you, isn't it?"

"Yes."

"Why?"

"I can't go into all the gory details."

"There's no one to help, no family money, nothing put away for a rainy day?"

"It's been raining for four years, all the money's gone. I'm sorry Nick, you didn't expect sadness."

"Don't be silly," he said, placing his hands on the back of my neck and massaging the tense muscles.

"I hadn't realized how ground down I've become, how close to falling apart. The only thing that has gotten me through the daily horror has been sheer will power, the desire to live at any cost, but now, in these last months, I feel I'm losing that energy."

Nick brought me a cup of coffee, his face set and serious. I was touched. I had not bargained for tenderness.

"Gambling's dangerous enough for all sorts of reasons, but it's positively lethal if you really need the money," he said.

"I don't have much choice," I said, and turned the conversation toward Nick. "How long have you been playing seriously?"

"About four years. I'd played occasionally, of course, in Vegas and the Caribbean, but the easy availability of Atlantic City has made gambling my avocation."

"How're you doing overall, since you first started?"

"I'm ahead about forty thousand dollars."

"That's very good."

"I've also had losing streaks during these years, and I sweated out those times. At this point the magazine subsists on these jaunts so I'm very careful. I've always known when to stop."

"You mean altogether?" I said.

We laughed at the absurdity of the question. "Who could resist all this fun and action?" he said.

"You've succeeded in taking yourself to the financial edge. Are you hoping that some event will take you the emotional edge too?" I asked.

"You go too far, Lily," he said.

"Having been born at the top, you gave it all away to better serve your life as a writer."

"It certainly looks that way, doesn't it?" said Nick. "I placed it all on the line when I bought the magazine and continued to pour more money into it. I could, I suppose, have chosen a simpler life, living off capital and clipping coupons. I doubt if I'll ever starve, but you're right, I placed it all on the line with the magazine."

"I envy you," I said.

"That's strange Lily. I envy you too. You seem to be living in a crush of grand opera emotion."

"It's very hard," I said.

"I don't imagine it's easy, but it is *grand*," he said. "And why do you envy me?"

"I envy you your youth."

"You're not much older."

"It's not the actual years. I'd love to go back in time -- begin again, with everything still before me, my life *tabula rasa*, all my mistakes still to come. I've wasted so much time. I'd love to be a writer. I envy that most of all."

"Did you ever try writing?" he asked.

"Early in my marriage I did -- short stories, poems and even half a novel. But I haven't looked at it for a long time. That unfinished book haunts me. Sometimes I dream that it projects itself out of the closet and into my hands to be finished."

I met Nick's eyes and could no longer bear to continue the conversation. I was becoming debilitated by the intrusion of reality.

"Let's snort some coke and get to the tables," I said. "I've only a few hours to play."

"Take the money and run, Lily. You've been very lucky both in the Bahamas and here, considering that you don't count cards and have never played before. You've won a fortune in three sessions. If you play now, you risk losing. That's not a good idea before you leave for home. It's depressing."

"I'll be careful, I won't play for high stakes. I'll coast."

"The cards can turn with an implacable ferocity, Lily". Said Nick, echoing Jake's exhortation.

We snorted coke and I recaptured the sense of renewal which I had felt after the shower, exaggerated now into an immensely bright, vibrant euphoria. During our conversation I had become vaguely aware of a slow-swelling coil of pressure that only one activity could slake or diminish. And then, in a bright, split second of clarity, instantly lost, I knew that I'd been moving toward this, from the moment I'd been awakened by the ringing of the telephone. I would use the white powder to draw a magic circle, which would keep the wolves of consciousness at bay.

Nick, in a moment of expansive elation, promised to drive me back to New York. He would spend the night with friends and drive up to Cambridge in the morning to teach his class. I accepted his offer and we concluded our hotel business, checked out and stored our luggage.

In the space of twenty-four hours, I had been catapulted into drugs, promiscuity and high-stakes gambling. I waited for a rush of revulsion, self-loathing and guilt, but instead, there was the sense of expanding, living up to some strange potential. For good or evil, I was moving forward; keenly aware that under cocaine's euphoria lay a small, clear kernel of truth. If I had graduated into degradation, it was an attainment still. I was at last, becoming. Ravenous for excitement, I sensed that my inordinate passion for pleasure would keep me alive.

CHAPTER FIVE

We entered the casino, agreeing that the day's watchword would be caution. We positioned ourselves at adjacent twenty-five dollar tables in the center of the room. I played for a while but couldn't recapture the excitement of the previous night. I wasn't betting enough for a total engagement of sensation, for that gratifying balance of tension and release. In gambling, less is considerably less. In fact, it's almost nothing.

The table was crowded with Sunday players using two or three hundred dollars of hard-earned table money for the weekend entertainment. Laborers mainly, the men had rough, stained hands and misshapen nails. Under garish make-up, the women's faces were exhausted, hair graying at the roots. They seemed more than content to pay a high price for this release from their daily burdens.

I forced myself to be patient and concentrate on the cards until I was significantly ahead. Then, increasing my bets, I hit an exhilarating stride. Riding the cards, I knew that the thrill of playing was derived from the leap, the escalation, as well as the win.

After a while, the cards turned and I lost steadily. I reduced my bets and still continued to lose. Down about a thousand dollars, in an attempt to recoup my losses, I broke my first, self-imposed rule by making the gambler's classic gesture of hubris: while losing, I bet on the come.

There was a sudden crowd gathering, a riveting of eyes and a hush of shared, vicarious excitement as I placed ten one hundred dollar bills on the table. My first card was a nine, against the dealer's ten. I got an ace and the dealer a ten, giving us both twenty. Not a very auspicious beginning.

The next hand was torture; two aces against the dealer's nine. The indicated play was to split aces, which meant betting another thousand dollars. In a slow-motion agony, I reached into my bag and extracted another thousand dollars. Everything stopped as I fumbled clumsily, each second prolonging the tension. Finally the money was found, counted and transformed into ten black chips, which I placed beside the first stack.

I'd been playing for only minutes and was down a thousand dollars. Now I was risking an additional thousand. So much for a careful beginning and vows of caution. The cards began to move and the dealer placed a three and a four diagonally across each ace; I'd received the worst possible cards.

With a wretched inner shrinking, I watched the ballet of hands. The dealer opened his cards to reveal a seven under the nine. He had a sixteen and would have to take an additional card.

It was only when the audience burst into cheers that I saw the dealer's next card. It was a ten. The dealer had busted! I'd won back my initial thousand and was ahead another thousand. The crowd roared.

Attracted by the noise, Nick came over, looked at my stacked chips and kissed my cheek.

"You've been betting too high, Lily," he said. "Remember our blood oaths on caution?"

The next second, however, he flashed me a smile, a bright accolade of victory. Heroism comes cheaply in a casino. The band of admirers remained, watching the progression of my luck. They were tapped out players, those unfortunate ones who, early on, had lost their stakes and now enjoyed the game vicariously, attracted by the victory of another, until fate changed its course and they were lured away by the new favorite.

"Keep 'em coming, you're hot, lady," said a voice.

"Go get it, bet it, don't back off," someone else urged.

Other voices, picking up the momentum, urged me on, like a Greek chorus, out of the action yet having a symbolic stake in the outcome of the game.

I ordered a popular gambler's drink, Kahlua and cream, an adult version of mother's milk. It seemed to soothe an inner rawness. Wearing the mantle of the conqueror, I played on, armed with the battle cries of the defeated, cheering me on to a victory, which might have belonged to them.

The Chorus acceded to my losses with philosophical resignation; the winning was cheered with high good humor, proof that Fortune can bestow blessings with the same lavishness as it bestows grief. The implacable fates have to rest sometime and why not on a cold Sunday afternoon in January, at the edge of sea in Atlantic City?

Unnerved by my initial, quick loss, I was now quite content to play one unit, resting after my exhausting sprint. Suddenly, slicing through the casino's din and my euphoria, shocking me with fear, I heard my name paged on the loud speaker. I was at the phone in seconds. It was Paul.

"Sorry to interrupt your weekend. I know how much it means to you"

"What's happened?" I said.

"Selena's on her way home from school. She's worried about me, I think. She asked permission to take a leave of absence. I told her to come home for a few days. But now that she's on her way, I don't think I can cope."

"Don't worry, I'll handle it. I'm on my way home. How are Annie and Kitty?"

"I spoke to Kitty when Selena called, she's fine. Annie's busy with her friends. It's good she's reliable, since I can't seem to remember anything. She calls, gets home on time, does her homework. Secretly, she's in charge of me, instead of the reverse."

There was silence on the other end of the phone. "You haven't asked me how I've been doing," I said finally.

"You'd have told me if you were winning."

His anticipation of bad news took the edge off my surprise.

"I've won," I said, suddenly near tears.

"That's good," he said, uninterested.

"I won eleven thousand dollars," I shouted.

"Have you?"

"Yes, I have."

"I'm glad for you."

"It's for you, too," I said, "it's for us."

"I know, thank you."

"Is it very bad?" I asked, my anger transformed to pity.

"As bad as it's ever been."

"I'm leaving right this minute. I'll be home on the next bus. Hold on."

I was grateful that I had almost three hours to prepare myself for what awaited me. I told Nick about Paul's call and that I had to leave immediately.

"I'll take the bus," I said, "they leave every hour on Sunday. Please stay, don't drive me back."

"It would be my great pleasure to drive you home," he said.

We left the casino quickly.

I got out at the bus station to buy sodas. The large overheated room was filthy and littered, filled with derelicts, wine-smelling and evil looking. The stench of rancid fried food from an adjacent restaurant and the smell of urine, overpowering. Holding my breath, I ran out, not stopping for the sodas, unwilling to breathe vile air. I fled into the comfort and warmth of the car.

I opened the window, sprayed cologne on my hands and before we hit the highway, lit a joint, inhaling the sweet, pungent odor of the grass, waiting for the haze to descend. In a few minutes I saw the landscape as a mindless blur.

"Is it a good idea for you to smoke grass now?" he asked. "Your phone call was obviously a summons."

"Sometimes it's essential to be disassociated," I said. "It's very hard to come in from outer space without decompressing in some neutral territory. If I don't do this the crash will be devastating."

"Is your life so awful then?" Nick asked, his tone skeptical. "You seem to have everything, beauty, intelligence, charm, family and a measure of mobility."

I considered his words silently, trying to visualize the person he described.

"You know, Lily, a bad marriage is as common as air. Are you sure you're not over-dramatizing it?"

"I wish I were," I said, as he placed his hand over mine. "If you take me at all, you must take me on faith."

"On faith," Nick said, solemnly echoing the toast of the previous night. He seemed supremely young then, and I knew that to be with Nick was to be touched by the reflected light of his youth and its implicit hope.

"I once read something that chilled my heart," I said.

"What?"

"Whatever happens also happens to one's children."

I became increasingly silent as we neared the city. The disappointing end of the joy ride that I had intuited was reflected in the palpable gloom of Eighth Avenue's Sunday night desolation. We drove further uptown and when we stopped at a traffic light, I saw, in the distance, the square, stolid, familiar outline of my apartment building. I felt a clutch of fear, a sensation of blind panic. I asked Nick to stop and he pulled over to the curb. The motor was still running, like some animal eager to be moving again.

We opened the window and I put my head down, breathing deeply, fighting faintness, blackness and nausea. After a few minutes, I revived and began to repair my ravaged face, arranging an altered expression, the picture that would be most familiar and comforting to my family.

Watching my transformation, Nick smiled faintly. Before I applied lipstick, he leaned over, tilted my face toward his and kissed me. Astonishingly, I quickened to him and our embrace became sexual. The street lamp shone upon us, illuminating our set piece of lovers parting.

As we drove the remaining blocks, my fear was now mingled with the sharp, inappropriate sensation of physical arousal. I remembered the premature death of a beloved friend, the gnawing, unappeasable sorrow at the wake, the burning eyes and throat from weeping and then the sudden, shocking burst of violent sexuality toward a stranger, who, meeting my impulse, moved with me in one gesture of frenzy into the bathroom where we locked the door and fell upon each other, prey to our precipitous sorrow, clinging and groping in a savage reaffirmation of life. It was only the insistent knocking at the door that restrained us from consummating our instant, inchoate desire.

I alit from the car, walking swiftly, my heart throbbing with terror and thrill, feeling the pressure of Nick's lips and hands on my body, an invisible shield against the darkness.

CHAPTER SIX

The apartment was ablaze with lights and totally silent. I walked through in search of signs of life.

Selena's duffel bag, books and scarf were strewn across the floor of her room, a smoked cigarette was in the ashtray and an empty soda can on its side. She had come home. Turning to leave, I saw a note propped up on the bureau.

I'm sorry--so very sorry--what can I say? I love you always -- no matter what -- please know that -- please try to be sure of that, if nothing else as regards to me--

I am unfortunately sick, and have been for a very long time -- I have less and less control. I am on an emotional elevator -- up and down, down and up...

There was no reason for me to get so angry. It's no excuse to say that I am sick. It's no good saying I'm sorry.

Perhaps I can say please just try to forgive me -- even if you don't understand it.

Daddy.

He was, through everything, still eloquent. I regretted having left my post as sentinel. During my absence, the territory had been invaded and war declared. Making love to another man seemed a venial sin; leaving the castle unguarded was a mortal one.

I went into the kitchen. From the unused maid's room in the rear came a moan of despair. I walked to the closed door and stopped.

"Paul, are you all right?"

"Yes," he said, "don't come in, please."

"Come out and talk to me then."

"Soon." A deep sob tore the air. I retreated to the bedroom and placed the money in stacks on the bureau. The sight of my victory cheered me. It was a disreputable glory but one to be lifted out of the debris of life and polished to a high patina.

I went to the window and looked at Central Park in its bare, wintry elegance. Sliding from under bands of loose, swiftly moving clouds, an iridescent silver moon rippled the lake with a hard gleam and was gone.

I drank in this lunar beauty as life's blood, and prayed for courage. I waited for Paul in the living room. After a few minutes, I heard his slow, hesitant tread in the hallway.

"I'm here," I called.

Huddled over and shivering, Paul walked through the connecting doors. In spite of the warmth of the apartment, he was wearing several sweaters, a thick wool robe and a scarf. He was hugging himself, struggling against some great inner cold.

"What happened?" I asked.

He lifted his head and I looked into his ravaged face, the eyes filled with a grief that turned me to stone. All my preparations for battle had been useless, I was routed, demolished at the first skirmish.

Finally he spoke.

"When Selena arrived, full of herself and her adolescent misery, I simply couldn't listen. I was sick and depressed as usual, minding my own ghastly business. Everything quickly escalated into screaming and accusations. I shouted, threatened, and drove her out of the house with Annie tracking behind. It's my fault. I have no judgment, no control. I'm too weak and depleted, Lily."

Paul turned his face toward mine, and like the Ancient Mariner, repeated a terrible litany.

"I wake in the morning and with the first flicker of consciousness, I feel a scream begin to form deep inside me, and then I run, barely able to make it to the bathroom. I turn on the shower full blast, and howl into a towel, so that no one will hear."

I had risen to the sound of Paul's unbearable agony for years and had often heard him recite its horrors again in the evening.

"You can't know how it feels, Lily, and thank God you'll never know."

"No, I've never felt that way," I said. I was aware, however, of a constant shadow of fear, that his calamity would befall me. Anything was possible.

"The pills aren't working," I said. "You must see the doctor again immediately."

"Do you really think the doctor can do anything, that he knows anything? They're all just guessing, and I'm their guinea pig. The pills are as horrendous as the illness."

He was right. They had made him twitchy, lethargic and even more deeply depressed. And those were only the immediate effects. The long-term reverses had yet to emerge.

Paul was roused to anger at the mention of his "tormentors," as he termed the long string of doctors he had consulted. He could no longer function without the pills and he felt that he should never have begun to take them. They had disturbed a precarious balance, which might have adjusted itself naturally.

Exhausted by a burst of emotion, he sat down on the couch and put his arms around me, his head on my shoulders. I was keenly aware of my own emotional see-saw, moving from pity to a place beyond compassion, where resentments, banked like fires, were ready to flame into fury at the slightest conflict.

Stiffening my small reserve of resilience, I was careful not to cross the small, dwindling space that separated us. The power of his grief was annihilating and I was frightened looking into his face so familiar that it seemed my own. Sensing my resistance, he sat up and moved to the other end of the sofa.

"You look tired, Lily," he said.

"Yes," I said, relieved to change the subject.

The violent egotism of the depressed permits no other interests.

"I was working hard at the blackjack tables."

"Did you win?"

"Don't you remember? I told you on the phone that I'd won eleven-thousand dollars."

"Oh, yes."

"We're ahead thirty-thousand from my winnings. It'll keep us afloat and I intend to go on and win more."

"It won't help me. Nothing can help me."

"Yes it will," I said standing up, hating him for his illness and myself for my need of him. He wasn't there for me any longer and hadn't been for a very long time. Yet after all the years, I still looked to him, for approval, love, succor and admiration. When none came, I was always bewildered. It was a lesson I could not learn. For him I had gone from being a wife to a mother a long time ago.

"Do you think I'll make it back, Lily?"

"Yes, of course," I said.

*   *   *

He was at the window, outlined against the trees and the black sky, a figure in a Renaissance painting, eclipsing the landscape.

"I've been given every gift," he said, smiling ruefully and revealing perfect, white teeth.

And in truth he was right. The bitter, ironic Fates, having lavished beauty, intelligence, charm and physical prowess upon Paul, then adding the trappings of wealth and power, had vanquished them all with a single curse. Tears filled my eyes at the cruelty and waste.

"I'm tired," I said. "I haven't slept much."

"I'm sorry to cause you this pain, Lily. If you ever can, forgive me." He covered his face with his hands.

The doorbell rang. I wiped my eyes and composed myself.

"Pull yourself together, the children are back."

In the adjacent foyer, I opened the front door, beaming a welcome toward the sullen, self-righteous faces of Selena and her staunch acolyte, Annie.

"Hello, darlings," I said, taking each of them by the hand and pulling them to the bedroom door. "I've got something great to show you, close your eyes."

A veteran of adolescent wars, I knew that the best defense is a diversion.

"You haven't heard why I've come home," Selena said, preferring to remain the injured victim.

"We'll talk later. First I want to show you something." I grabbed the piles of green bills stacked on the bureau and tossed them in chaotic splendor over the entire bed. "Ready!" I cried, guiding them into the room with their eyes closed. "Look!" I said.

"Oh, oh," they chorused.

"Is it real?" asked Annie, the skeptic.

"Of course it's real," said Selena. "But is it ours?"

"I won eleven-thousand dollars," I said, "and it's both real and ours." I presented them each with a fifty-dollar bill.

"Oh Mom, the first time you won I thought it was just luck, but now -- you've really figured out a way, haven't you," Selena said.

"Yeah, you're real cool, Mom," Annie added, giving me the ultimate parental accolade.

"It's not as if I'd won a prize or done anything serious," I said.

"Wild blood runs in our veins," Selena said. "Wait till my friends hear this one, my mother, the gambler."

Selena was at an age when wild blood was the passport to the unknown, romantic world for which she felt herself destined.

"Take Kitty her fifty dollars when you go back up to school," I said. "By the way, how long are you staying?"

"A few days, I'm not sure," said Selena. "We have to talk right away, Mom."

"There's a note for you that I think you should read before we talk, it's on your bureau."

"I'll be right back," she said.

I was relieved that there was time to compose myself to cope with Selena's complicated emotions, to distinguish the real reason for her return from the putative one. I knew that I would have to muster the strength to listen quietly.

I lit a cigarette, willing myself calm, but my mind was flooded with myriad tormenting worries I'd repressed in Atlantic City. They came at me like a tidal wave: Kitty's irresponsibility, Selena's anger, and Annie's premature seriousness. And crying bouts, accidents, broken teeth, misplaced medications, over-compensations, lost glasses, school probations, airplanes, unadjusted braces, lost retainers. I though of teeth rotting, roots exposed, botulism lurking in cans of salmon, undiagnosed illnesses, rape, burst appendix, exams cut, classes missed, snipers, hitchhiking, the inevitable betrayal of friends, sex, boyfriends, cars, unworn seat belts, pregnancy, drunken driving, loneliness, war, drugs, overdoses, tight shoes, no arch supports, muggings, swimming in dangerous waters, sharks, lost ski gloves, frostbite, lockjaw, abortions, torn boots, missed vaccine shots, Vitamin C deficiencies, smoking, old muscular injuries, broken bones, the loss of love, rejection, repression, their secret lives and the great, overwhelming fear for their father.

Selena entered the bedroom draped in a purple towel, her long golden hair cascading over her white arms. She seemed to draw in all the color of the room, a tableau embodying life in the soft, child-red of her lips and the clear gray of her eyes.

"I made up with Daddy," she said, "and he's gone to sleep."

Since our return from the Bahamas, Paul had elected to sleep in the study. My nightly insomnia disturbed him.

Selena looked at me and smiled a secret signal, which told me that the frantic emotions were being stilled and she was free to accept my total love.

"We'll talk tomorrow, I'm tired, Mommy," she said, resting her soft cheek against mine.

I turned off the light and lay in the darkness, touching my face, breathing the scent of skin, feeling the blunt texture of nails and soft fingertips, tracing the unknown shape of my features, posing the mute question: who will mother the mothers?

I awoke the next morning, alone, on a bed littered with money, having dreamed that I had assumed the role of an infamous courtesan. Reluctantly slipping into my own life, I saw it was early enough for a quiet cup of coffee before the day began. I headed to the front door for the newspaper, and in the hallway, hazily passing the dining room, I glimpsed an unfamiliar shadow. Turning, I saw, to my immense astonishment, that the entire room had changed.

Furniture, paintings and familiar objects had been removed and replaced by others from different parts of the apartment. The rug that had been under the dining table was gone, leaving a faded imprint on the wooden floorboards.

Moving trance-like into the study, I faced the same distorted images. Alien pieces of furniture were oddly arranged. The books, formerly organized by subject, were newly categorized by height, creating aggressive abstract shapes and making strange shelf-fellows. Every dust jacket had been removed.

The records were alphabetized regardless of category, Beethoven following hard upon the Beatles. All surfaces had been stripped of magazines, ashtrays, pictures and plants. It was a minimalist's dream and totally spotless.

The living room where I'd sat with Paul just hours before was unrecognizable. The mantle was bare. Gone were family pictures. Vases had vanished, candlesticks flown, rugs had been magically transported. Individuality was erased. It could have been a room in any first class hotel rather than a home.

Shocked and speechless, I entered the kitchen. Except for the large, immovable appliances, it was in the same state as the rest of the house. Nothing was the same. Huge cartons were brimming with discarded items. Counters were empty of all ordinary kitchen utensils, and when my eyes fastened on the space reserved for the coffee pot and it no longer occupied its customary position, I began to scream.

"What's wrong?" Paul said, his voice coming from the laundry room. He was on the top rung of a ladder, adjusting shelves, which had lain for years waiting to be bracketed. The laundry room had always been filled with old skis, broken tennis rackets, luggage, massive boxes of detergents, light bulbs, cans of coke and beer, cases of toilet paper, endless jars of jam, relish and chutney. It was the repository of a lifetime's accumulation of junk.

This generalized, familiar mess was now transformed into a room, which would have warmed the heart of the most exacting housewife. Shelved from floor to ceiling, boxes matched in size and weight, items categorized, labeled and placed in neat rows. The transformation was truly Herculean, a cleaning of our own Augean Stables.

"Where's the coffee pot?" I croaked in a voice barely recognizable.

"It's in the cupboard under the sink," he said. "I'll get it for you, Lily. There's no need to scream."

He climbed down the ladder and for a moment we faced each other. He was wearing a blue warm-up suit, a white towel wrapped around his neck. His face glowing from recent exertion, eyes bright and clear. A handsome, smiling, normal face. Like the apartment, Paul had been transformed.

"You were running?" I asked incredulously. "You haven't run in six months!"

"Well, I ran today, all the way up to the reservoir at about six AM. It was great. I did three miles and I feel wonderful."

His voice was firm, his movements sharp and sure. We stood in the laundry room in one of those great, silent moments, when reality, unbearably laden, becomes a dream. Although I couldn't understand, I saw us then, as if already distanced by time, like an old, vivid memory, watching but unable to fully comprehend or alter events.

I was in an old, torn tee-shirt of Paul's, barefoot, cold, unwashed, disheveled, coffee-deprived, clutching my hair with both my hands, body rigid with hysteria, face twisted with rage. Paul was elegant, poised, caught in the midst of fruitful labor, robust, active and normal.

It was my worst nightmare. Like everything else in the apartment, we, too, had changed places. I had become Paul.

"What've you done?" I whispered. And then louder: "What have you done?"

"Keep your voice down, Lily, you'll wake the kids. You're always complaining about the mess and now it's all perfectly arranged. Why are you so angry?" He seemed genuinely puzzled.

"My God," I wailed. "Why is everything changed?"

"I've cleaned everything up," he said.

"It's clean but it's crazy," I said, clutching a vase and a painting I'd extracted from the carton, proof of the madness. I waved them in Paul's face.

"Why did you throw these out?"

"I wasn't throwing them out, I was putting them away. We never use these things, they're just dust collectors."

"They belong here, I love them," I cried.

"Stop whining, Lily, everything still belongs to you, they're just in cartons for the moment."

"Why did you remove all the dust jackets?"

"Uniformity."

I grabbed Paul's arm and pulled him through the apartment.

"Where are the pictures, mirrors, candlesticks? What have you done with everything? How on earth did you manage to move and change things around alone? Why is the furniture arranged in this bizarre fashion? Why?"

"Please calm down, Lily. I can explain."

"You never asked me," I cried, "you just went ahead and changed everything."

"You were sleeping, I didn't want to disturb you."

"But why? *Why* did you do it?"

"I couldn't sleep last night," he said. "Usually the pills knock me out, but last night I became very agitated. Suddenly, I looked around at the clutter, all the inessential junk, and I thought how good it would be to finally get rid of it once and for all. So I cleared things out and then I wanted everything to be new and fresh again, like it was in the beginning, and that's when I changed everything around. I left the laundry room for last.

"You see, Lily, I couldn't stop moving. After being inactive for so long it felt so good to work. Then, when dawn came, I went out and ran, came back and started to work again. I've just finished." He looked at me for a response. "I thought you'd be pleased."

I lay my head on a counter and wept.

"I'll move everything back," Paul pleaded, "it'll take no time at all. I promise you, Lily, things will be as they were."

"They can never be as they were."

Huddling in a chair, I felt the waves of shock subsiding, and something far more ominous approaching. It was then that Paul turned, his face a Hyde-like grotesque, distorted with months of pent-up, self-lacerating rage. I froze.

"For God's sake, Lily," he said in a vicious sneer, "what's wrong with you? Stop sniveling about some sticks of furniture -- your precious things will be restored to their proper places."

He brought his face close to mine. "You're so God-damned bovine, content in your rut, hating change. You'd never move your ass if you didn't absolutely have to, *ever*. What's the matter with you? Can't you see progress? Can't you see something positive for a change? You're always suspicious. All I've done is move a few things around and you act as if I've tried to murder you.

"I've been hanging around here, on and off for years, barely able to tie my shoe laces, crying and moaning, steadily driving everyone crazy, and finally, I'm able to do something positive and the queen is displeased, the queen is not amused.

"Let me tell you something my house-proud lady, today, after months of idleness, I'm going to go to work and start making money again."

Paul moved his right hand back in a tennis forehand, smashing at an imaginary ball.

"While I was cleaning, I could feel my mind working again, ideas flowing, like in the old days. Pieces of puzzles clicked into place. I was on top of it all again. I remembered an idea that I'd discarded. If I were able to excite interest, I'd raise money and sell large, cheap tracts of land for minimal investment, tax write-off stuff. I'd have to work fast, against time, since there's very little money left.

"I'll hire two secretaries, a day and night shift, get additional phones, rent typewriters, stock up on food, sleep on the couch. If I bring a change of clothes, I won't even have to come home. I'll shower in the bathroom. Since I'll be working against time, I'll require seed money. Yes, I'll have to invest in myself again. There's no other choice. I can't get a job, you've seen that. I'm too old, over-qualified. I've never worked for anyone, ever. Besides, you've just made a killing at the tables, and that'll keep us for a while. We're off and running again, Lily."

My fears crystallized. The frenetic activity, rage simmering beneath the surface, rapacious viciousness, volcanic flow of ideas and superhuman energy announced the menace that was now here. Paul had flipped into mania.

I escaped to the bedroom knowing that I had to marshal my forces, which at the moment seemed pitifully weak. I was racked with self-hate at my impotence in the face of Paul's illness. All the torment we had suffered was for nothing. It had made no difference. Paul controlled me and now he would give no quarter. He'd continue to control the money and me. I was his lifeline.

In his manic phase, Paul was a genius at ruse and concealment, and I was no match for him. I didn't know how much money we had left, nor where it was kept, and I'd never known. I had only Paul's word for everything. His stock manipulations, financial ventures and all business dealings were hidden from me. He would not leave and give me peace, and I could not leave. There was simply no exit.

Yet I knew that I must find and learn to use that which I had rarely touched in myself -- independence, courage and a determination to survive at all costs. Along with Sloth, Vanity and the other seven sins, I had been given the gift of hope. Against odds, circumstance and reason, an ancient magic passed through bloodlines by women who had lived before me, endured violent vicissitudes and prevailed. Shivering with animal terror, I prayed for animal endurance.

Annie and Selena, yawning, wrapped in their comforters, entered the bedroom.

"Have you seen the apartment?" Annie asked. "It looks weird but great. Daddy turned it upside down."

"It gives the place a real lift," Selena added. "Daddy's going to start working again. He's better and he's going to start a new business."

"Yes, he told me Selena," I said. "After Annie goes to school, we can have our talk."

"I'd love to Mom, but I'm going up with Annie today to see the old school, hang out and take the bus back tonight."

At least there was some benefit from Paul's seeming recovery. I had expected a cross examinations, anger, resentment and rebellion. Selena's fears were temporarily allayed and her return to school would lessen my burden.

I went to a bank downtown and deposited my winnings in a money-market account. When I arrived home, most of the furniture and paintings had been restored to their original places. Files and an overnight bag lay beside the front door. Anxious to avoid further confrontation with Paul, I busied myself in the kitchen and attempted to establish calm with work.

Paul entered the kitchen resplendent in a gray striped double-breasted suit, blue shirt and silver tie. His Saville Row elegance and beauty were astonishing. In the luminescent glow of mania he was, like a film star, larger than life, exuding force and power. The only evidence of what was lurking beneath his physical magnificence was his smile, brilliant and ferocious, the smile of an ardent murderer.

"You look well."

"Thank you," he said, waiting for more. "Aren't you going to wish me luck?"

"Of course, Paul. Good luck."

"I think I'll make it now. At least I'm going to try. I'm going to give it everything. It's my last shot."

He spoke quietly, conversationally.

"You know," I said, "all of this movement, this extreme activity, do they seem inappropriate to you Paul?"

"Do they seem so to you?"

"They reflect the symptoms of a certain behavior."

"What behavior?"

"Mania."

Paul burst out laughing.

"You're really a pain in the ass, Lily. Do you know that, my dear pampered wife? That you're a pain in the ass?"

"Dr. Elster described these symptoms often enough," I said, trying to ignore his words and the ugly, sarcastic tone in which they were delivered. "He was very careful to let us know how important it was that he be called immediately, by either one of us. You agreed to that, Paul, and now you really must tell him how you're behaving so he can adjust the medication. It's for your own benefit, Paul, you know that."

"And if I don't call him and do what you say, you'll be on the blower as soon as I leave the apartment to file your report to the Commissioner of My Brain, right?"

"You were in the office when Dr. Elster said it was most important to call the moment I noticed any manic symptoms; you agreed it was an excellent idea."

"But I also know that after months of misery, I feel better today. I want to work and I feel capable of working again. You will not, do you hear, Lily, you will not call Dr. Elster until I see him on my regular appointment next week."

"But Paul, don't you know..."

He grabbed my wrist and twisted it behind me, his fingers biting into my flesh, the pain flooding my arm.

"Stop!" I screamed.

"I gather then that you're going to listen to me," Paul snarled.

"Yes, yes."

He released my arm. Weeping tears of humiliation and pain, I turned away so that he could not see my face and further fuel his fury.

"You've never listened to me, Lily, but you'd better listen now. You've never done what I wanted, not in the important things, and you'd better begin." He moved his face to my ear and spat the words in my face. "Listen! And stop that God-damn crying!" A wail of agony escaped me but he roared on. "And I mean now!"

"Let me out, Paul," I begged, "release me from this marriage before I'm as sick as you are, and the children will have no one."

"If you want out, *you* get out!"

"The children need someone to be in charge, and you can't do that."

"I'll do it," he thundered, banging his fist through a wood cabinet.

"You hate me, Paul, let me out."

"I don't want to leave my home. If I wanted to, I couldn't leave. We have no money."

"I'll die if you stay."

"Have no fear, Lily, you're too placid to die of grief, and much too egotistical. Cows don't die of grief."

"All you need me for is a scapegoat, someone to control, and I'm the only person that you still have that power over. I'm all that's left of your kingdom of serfs. You've got to let go of me. Give me a divorce, a separation, anything!"

"You're caught like a rat in a trap, and I'm going to torture you to death."

Paul bared his teeth and loosed a death's head grin. I crumpled to the floor, keening, shrieking like an animal.

Paul pulled me up, slapped me hard with his open hand, back and forth until my face flamed and my neck burned with unbearable pain. The slaps echoed across the tiled kitchen and in my own ears, vibrating into a low hum until the silence was as absolute as my defeat.

"Till death do us part." Paul's voice dripped venom.

And then he was gone.

I lay a long time on the cold floor. And then, in that moment of utter defeat, alone, bereft, tormented, brutalized and beaten, I heard from deep within my soul, inevitable words of simple certainty; a solemn vow. This will never happen to me again.

CHAPTER SEVEN

The next weeks brought an avalanche of anxieties. The children's lives were beset by emotional crises, academic failings and probation at school.

Annie, the genial bedrock of good will had become morose, ill-tempered, rebellious and finally ill with a raging fever. The temperamental fluctuations continued after the illness, signaling her belated entrance into true adolescence. Within a matter of weeks she was transformed from a sweet, obedient child into a virago of resentment.

The Dean summoned me to Kitty and Selena's school. They were on the verge of being expelled. As the cab drew up, I saw two slight, coatless figures braving the February cold, hands clasped, faced puffed with misery, long flags of red and gold hair waving in the winter wind, auguring war. The gentle landscape of Massachusetts became our battlefield, exploding with scenes, tears and recriminations.

The conferences with teachers, deans and administrators were conducted with gravity fit for a purge trial. It seemed that we were deciding nothing less than the fate of the world. Finally, after much soul searching, the offenders were temporarily reprieved. Selena and Kitty would remain at school on probation. I was relieved to know that they would be safe under house arrest.

Days were spent battling the school; nights were given over to more personal wars. Although a seasoned veteran of familial strife, I was daunted by my children's youthful vigor. Their verbal assaults were painful. They mined the trivial and the significant haphazardly, keeping me off balance. Problems of oily hair interspersed with difficulties concentrating; fears for their father and their futures following hard upon a deep dread of expanding thighs. Withstanding the monumental rage of three daughters, I became convinced that an army of fifteen-year-old girls, properly led, could conquer and rule the world.

*   *   *

In the ensuing weeks a silence heavier than stone lay between Paul and me. Paul worked without sleep, traveled constantly, spent money uncontrollably and received an endless flow of purchases. I heard him dictating, typing and telephoning late into the night. The amount of his correspondence alone was staggering.

During the rare times Paul remained home he slept in the study. Our explanation to the children was that we were trying to ease the tension between us. But it was glaringly evident that we had become estranged. This marked separation, rather than cooling the enmity, served only to widen existing rifts. Indifference and cruelty became our way of communicating.

Constantly on the alert for confrontation, we met late one night in the kitchen. Sleepless and emotionally raw, we spewed venom, not speaking but rather hissing, braying, roaring, grunting, using whatever sound best expressed our bestial antipathy toward one another.

My request for a separation punctuated every encounter, causing Paul to fly into a rage.

"Never, I'll never leave. This is my home and if you can't live with me, get out! Get out!"

Paul's anger had always destroyed me. Keeping everything rosy was my profound ambition, and I never hesitated to lie and cheat to insure his favor. My traditional familial role was to accept blame abjectly, apologize profusely, loathing myself as I groveled for peace. Paul's anger, exacerbated by his illness, flared at a delayed mail arrival, a misplaced newspaper, and was invariably vented toward me. Now, for the first time, I began to inure myself to his wrath.

The habits of shared intimacy were deeply engrained. The complicated history of our married life and love was too powerful for sudden emotional independence. It was as if my mind had grown onto Paul's like a grafted tree, having no distinct root of its own.

It was only after the scene in the kitchen that I experienced a dim, nascent sense of otherness, and became vividly aware of a long-hidden truth. Paul had abandoned me when he became ill. I had been truly alone for years.

*　　*　　*

One day, he called unexpectedly from the office. It had been more than a month since we had spoken.

"How are you, Lily?" he asked softly. The timbre of his voice was changed and the abrupt, angry impatience was gone.

"Miserable."

"I've done it again, haven't I?"

"Yes."

"I'm so very sorry."

"You've been monstrous."

"I know and I can't even ask you to forgive me. It's unforgivable."

"Something has to change," I said. "I can't suffer and mourn every day, living on the edge. I've nothing left over to give to the children or myself. There has to be a time when even the most terrible tragedy is over. This eternal torment is unbearable. I want a life again."

"I can't tell you how sad I am for the way I've behaved, for the anguish I've brought upon you and the children. I've failed you all, emotionally and financially.

"Oh God, Lily, how cold, dreary and miserable our lives have become. And you were right, I've been manic. Today it all crashed down on me, again. I want to come home and talk. Please."

"Yes," I said. "We've got to talk."

I washed up, prepared sandwiches and brought them into the study. Paul had left the apartment in the morning, a youthful, vibrant man. He returned now, a few hours later, an old, defeated one. His lightning character transformations would have been the envy of the most accomplished actor.

We sat in the study facing each other in our accustomed corners. I placed a tray of food before him. We were silent for a long time. All the scenes had been played over and over again throughout the years in this room.

Paul rose and walked to where I sat, turned and looked toward the window, his eyes seeming to focus on something in the far distance. His hands grazed my cheek in an aborted caress and I flinched.

"You always used to sing in the house, you know, Lily."

"What are we going to do, Paul?" I asked.

He moved back to the sofa and lay his head on the back of it, staring at the ceiling.

"No, you can't live like this," he said. "No one can. I've made another terrible mistake. The pills shot me over the top. They pulled me out of depression only to thrust me into mania. I've been over-medicated once again. It's been a disaster. I was manic. Yes, I know you told me. Now, unfortunately, I know as well."

"Tell me the worst."

"I've lost money again."

"How much?"

"Twenty-five or thirty thousand."

"That's almost exactly the amount I won.

"Please Lily, keep calm."

"You never listen to anyone. Every time we're given another chance, you ruin it. Everything crashes down on us, worse than before. It's like the fucking house of Atreus, we are doomed."

"I'm the doomed one," Paul said quietly. "I've just come from Dr. Elster's office. He's given me new pills. They're good, they work quickly and he's optimistic that they're right for me."

"Dr. Elster was optimistic about the last pills. They were so good they made you manic. Then you're off and running and you don't want to change the dosage because after endless months of depression you finally feel better. I know the scenario."

"What shall I do, Lily, give up? I wouldn't mind. You always drag me up, urging me to try to live. You're a hope-junky, Lily."

"How much money do we have left."

"Enough for three months," he said, "if we're careful."

"Even after the last loss?"

"Yes."

"What's the plan now?"

"I've got to get off the present pills gradually and then wait a few weeks before I take the new pills. Then it's several weeks before they become effective."

"You mean you'll be without anything for weeks?"

"Yes."

"Oh God."

"Quiet, Lily," he warned. And I was silent. I'd learned that much at least.

"I'm the one who suffers withdrawal, not you. I can stay at a hotel or burrow in the old maid's room and stay out of everyone's way. I have to keep in close touch with Dr. Elster."

There was a silence during which I saw the long, tortuous way we had come and shuddered at what lay before us. I had the sense of being propelled closer to the abyss, the ground softening and the letting go becoming desirable, easy, like it must be for people freezing to death. A place of rest. I focused in on Paul again.

"You can't stay alone," I said, having lived through withdrawal with him many times before.

"I could try."

"Of course you'll stay here," I said, suddenly overwhelmed by an unutterable pity and the sense of what we had once been to each other. "We'll manage somehow. We have before."

He came over to me, turned my chin up and looked deeply into my eyes.

"And then, when I'm on my feet, I'll leave." I looked at him. "Yes," he said, "It's true, Lily. I'll go."

I remembered then, when we were newly married. Lying in bed holding each other, we had dreamed our life, imagined our unborn children and how we would grow old together. We talked always, never bored, sharing deepest thoughts and lightest wit. From the first we had been lovers and the best of friends, absorbed and dedicated to one another.

He brought me flowers and I baked soufflés, and once while I was showering, he jumped in fully dressed to announce his first financial success, kissing me wildly under the fall of water.

*   *   *

We lived in a cancer ward of the mind for seven weeks. In the early days Paul seldom left his room. The physical and mental suffering was literally blinding. Invariably dressed in several heavy robes with a scarf at his throat, he trembled with a cold that nothing could warm.

No longer able to read or even focus on television, I lay under the covers in my room, praying for surcease from the agony. His pain was unbearable, and I was beyond visiting or being seen. Instead, I spent whole days talking to friends on the phone. In large measure their affection and compassion sustained me.

For years, my life had been bound by pain and crisis. I was fascinated by and envious of ordinary, unimportant pleasures like baking a cake, visiting a museum or buying a gift. Far beyond riches or love, I desperately longed for a normal day.

To relieve the bleakness and isolation of those weeks, I turned to drugs. When the pressure of thoughts became unbearable, I'd smoke a joint and drift into dreams of pleasure and salvation. When I was immobilized by depression, I'd snort a line of coke, enabling me to carry on the basic chores of life with apparent vigor. Sleep was wooed with pills, which I permitted to seduce me nightly.

The anguish of those long dark days was broken by dreams of gambling. I played endless games of blackjack, winning effortlessly. These fantasies excited my imagination, comprising my one joy and escape. The desire to win, if only at cards, was a spark I kept alive.

It was then, in those hibernating weeks, that the telephone became my lifeline. A phone conversation was an artificial stage upon which I could perform, creating a semblance of real life. Bonnie entertained me with her chatter, and I lived vicariously through her social whirl as she presented me with the latest news of the Rialto.

Nick called frequently from Cambridge, talking books and sex. Jake called from Athens or Rio or Vegas and like Scheherazade, I spun stories to keep him on the line, flirting madly while lying in bed drugged, frazzled, unkempt, reasoning that the illusion of life was better than no life at all. I used the excuse of a lingering viral infection to explain my lethargy and immobility.

I was grateful that Kitty and Selena were up at school and spared the horror of our daily life. They were, of course, aware of Paul's present condition. Annie spent a good deal of time out of the house, visiting friends, staying overnight when possible. The children became stoic, repressed and sad.

At last, after about four weeks on the new pills, Paul gradually became active and started going to the office daily. He was quiet and withdrawn, but at least he had begun to work. Avoiding confrontation, we were careful to maintain a courteous, cautious distance.

One day, having depleted my stock of drugs and overcome by that most primitive of desires, the simple longing for another's touch, I called Nick and arranged to meet him in Atlantic City. Time was running out. I had to make some more money.

Boarding the bus at the Port Authority on a windy day in late March, I felt like Persephone returning from the underworld. To my ravenous soul, the mundane seemed dazzling. Scarves flowed, trees bent, newspapers spiraled, coats flapped and faces were whipped with color. I had come through a certain agony, alive still, and I felt a powerful surge of happiness and the deep resolve born of suffering. I would be one upon whom nothing is lost.

Lulled by the rhythmic cradling of the bus, I watched the winter twilight swiftly darken into night. Suddenly, illuminating the blackness in bright neon, a name flashed across the sky.

Johnny Messina
Appearing Nightly

I felt a flush of wild joy. The bus picked up speed on the flat of the road as if spurred by desire. It had been six months. Now, careening toward him while stars of light exploded his name across the sky in mythic extravagance, I thought how the ancients would have applauded this celestial announcement heralding passion.

CHAPTER EIGHT

Bursting into the hotel room, I dropped my suitcase and was at the phone before the door slammed shut. Wildly excited, I was gripped by a sense of speeding toward an inexorable fate.

Lighting a cigarette with trembling hands, I tried frantically to remember my alias if someone other than Johnny answered the phone. I was already following one of his immutable precepts: "Always lie."

The line rang interminably; each buzz tightened the coil of tension. Finally, the phone was lifted.

"Hello," Johnny said in his merry, sitting-on-top-of-the-world, entertainer's voice. I couldn't utter a word. "Hel-lo," he sang, anticipating pleasure, glowing with energy, riding a high of attention, compliments and adulation. Women's adulation. Jealousy strangled breath.

"Who's this?" he asked.

"Me."

"That voice," he said, turning an accusation into a caress. "Where are you?"

"Here."

"Alone?"

"Yes."

"When did you get here?"

"Now."

"I've got two shows. Later."

"Yes."

"One o'clock. Suite 108."

"Yes."

"And hurry."

"Yes."

"And hurry" -- that was an old joke. As if there was any chance I wouldn't fly to him as fast as I could.

Even if there was time, I rushed: showered, oiled, scented, sprayed, creamed, powdered, and dressed in minutes. I attacked taxis, drawing drivers into my obsession, pressing them until they, too, were consumed with the race. Every cab ride was an emergency and a second's lapse could drive me wild. If I didn't have correct change, I over tipped lavishly -- a twenty-dollar bill for a six-dollar fare. My spirit brooked no opposition, no waiting. I had to get there. "And hurry!"

I remembered then, all our meetings at strange hours in impossible places: musky motels, borrowed apartments, whorish hotels, dark bars, secret corners, special signals -- and always the terrible urgency of getting there.

Slipping in rain, sliding in snow, and once, on a steamy summer day, I abandoned a traffic-snarled cab under the blazing sun and ran, high heels tottering, reaching my destination flushed and victorious, dripping with sweat.

From first moment, Johnny had overwhelmed me. The air quickened with an electric charge, as if heavy with a sudden unseasonable heat. And now my resolve not to see him again had been vanquished by the mere sight of his name on a highway billboard.

The telephone rang, jolting me out of my reverie. It was Nick. I had forgotten him along with the rest of the world.

"I've just checked in. Shall I come up?"

I thanked providence and my caution that I had insisted on separate rooms.

"I'll meet you in the bar in half an hour."

"You sound nervous -- is anything wrong?"

"No. I want to shower and change. I'll see you soon."

For a moment I was seized with a sense of warring loyalties. And then I realized that I had none. Long ago, I had betrayed Paul with Johnny and had suffered keenly the abandonment of my marriage vows. The guilt was quickly submerged beneath the excitement and violent sexuality of our affair.

Inured to the damage wreaked upon others, we hurtled toward each other while victims fell by the wayside. His wife, my husband, eight children between us -- all cheated of our devotion and presence. Yet for me, no excuses mollified the wrong. Paul's drug-induced impotence, Johnny's rampant desire, his wife's implicit, tormented acceptance of his behavior -- nothing could not justify my actions or ease my guilt. The old *canard* that if it weren't me, it would be another had never fooled me. It was always me, and I always knew it.

And now, after all the years, I no longer had allegiances. I belonged to no one. It was a strange, exciting sensation with undiscovered possibilities. I had come a long way from absolutes.

Nick's presence in Atlantic City had, at first, seemed an impediment, but was now oddly stimulating. I was astonished at myself, delighted by the novelty of having no greater authority than my own inclinations, having no need of anyone's approbation. I was no longer burdened with moral responsibility. I was no longer anyone's darling.

Suddenly, my long-dormant sense of fun sprang to life, sharpened by the long weeks of soul-stultifying agony from which I had just emerged. Johnny and I had been magnetized by sexual passion, but it was our profound commitment to play that bound us with hoops of steel.

Once, in an opulent velvet and marble hotel suite, I lay naked on a satin bed, a glass of champagne in one hand, a joint in the other, caviar on a nearby pillow, while Johnny, damp and glowing from the shower, a towel wrapped around his waist, smiled at me and said, "You're just like a pig in shit, Lily," and wrapped his fresh, cool body around mine.

Now I smoked a joint, had a long scented bath followed by a short icy shower, donned black lace underwear and sheer black stockings. Before leaving the room, I looked at my reflection in the mirror. Excitement had burnished my skin, kohl-rimmed eyes glittered black, lips flashed copper and golden hair haloed the painted face. I looked like the Empress, a Tarot figure representing the temptations of the flesh.

I could scarcely believe that this shimmering creature sheathed in black jersey was the same woman who had lain in bed for weeks weeping.

*   *   *

I got off the elevator and was greeted by a life-sized photograph of Johnny, encased in glass. He was smiling as seductively as a woman. The darkly Italianate face, with its prominent brow and cleft chin, invited admiration.

The archetypal Mediterranean visage reflected a world where man is king, and woman his vassal. It was precisely because he embodied the qualities of his ancient blood, a direct masculine sensuality clear in its shape and promise, that he was so adored. No quarrels here with identity, liberation, equality. No barriers to the urgent expression of the polarity explicit in his sensual message. It was the mating game that Johnny sold so successfully; he was the peacock strutting unabashedly in open coquetry while the women flew around him, competing for his favors.

This ballad singer, attired in tuxedo and bow tie in place of tunic and tabard, echoed the troubadours, singing of love and passion in a language without equivocation. The paradigm of all he professed, secure in his values, unyielding in ideas and attitudes, he was a true primitive, like his ancestors who sang in ancient times on remote Sicilian shores.

From contemplating the glories of <u>Magna Grecia</u>, I was borne into the bar on a tide of frantic rock beats, wolf whistles and cat calls evocative of more ancient Dionysian rites, directly into the Anglo-Saxon, blue-eyed gaze of Nicholas Snow Van Pelt.

He was leaning against the bar where we had first had a drink, eager and earnest, smiling broadly. I sat down on a bar stool and he stood beside me.

"You're radiant, Lily. What've you been up to?"

"I've been south this winter. I've spent a season in hell."

"How did you escape?"

"I bribed Charon."

"Good job," he said, "Let's have a bottle of champagne."

"It's too expensive here," I said.

"I've just won a pile of money, and I'm celebrating a great coup," he said.

The band left, and soft, taped sentimental forties music filtered through an atmosphere thick with alcohol, tobacco, leather and humanity. We moved to a table facing the parade of people.

"You've been lucky for me, Lily," he said, placing his hand over mine. "Since we met things have been on an upswing. I came to the end of my inheritance about a year ago and since then I've been borrowing from friends and gambling to keep the magazine afloat. And now I've finally found a patron who'll give us money."

He paused, smiling, and brushed his fine white fingers lightly across my knuckles. "But how about you, Lily?" he asked. "I've missed you -- it's been nearly two months. You sounded fine on the phone, but I kept getting the feeling that you were on drugs. What was happening?"

Haltingly, I told him about the weeks of horror I'd been through.

"There was always the sense that I was sacrificing my life for Paul," I said. "Everything seemed joyless, impossible and doomed. Life had become misery and there were times when I didn't care if I lived or died. I don't want to feel that way again."

"No, of course not," said Nick, his pale face reflecting an empathy that I thought must derive from his own experiences of loss during childhood.

"I've chosen guilt at abandoning Paul instead of staying with him and giving up my life. I'm going to live and bear the guilt of leaving him."

"How about money?"

"He lost most of our meager resources in his last kamikaze flight into business. What I won will cover what he lost. There's no question that we have to pool our resources at this point. In essence, it's as if I'd won nothing. I'm starting from scratch but at least the money's under my name. How's that for freedom? How's that for independence? I get to keep my own money. I must be the last liberated woman in America."

"It's a step in the right direction anyway," he said.

"Yes. Now I just have to use it to win enough money to support my freedom."

The champagne arrived in a silver bucket and the waitress left it to cool.

"Playing with important money is bad enough," Nick said, "But playing with scared money is disastrous. You can't hope to be as lucky as you've been. If you continue to play for those stakes, you'll be killed."

"I don't have any alternative at the moment," I said. "I've got to support the girls while I look for a job. After that, I'll have to supplement my salary. I've never worked. Any job I get won't pay enough. I can't be independent without money. You've gambled with important money and won, Nick. You're ahead."

Nick looked uncomfortable.

"You can't trust a gambler's memory, Lily. We lie even to ourselves. I've been behind a great deal too. I'm ahead for the last year."

"And before then?"

"Up and down."

Nick didn't want to continue the conversation. The blackjack tables were too close to us here for absolute honesty.

"Counting's enormously helpful," I said. "You said so yourself and won a bundle last time."

"Counting gives the player an important edge," he said. "But there are other considerations: luck, self-control and the subliminal maneuvers of the unconscious. Luck is the great leveler. I began to win big the night we met and since then everything has gone well for me. I've won quite a bit today. I hope this great roll will last a long time, but the end, like death, is inevitable. There's no way to beat it. When the cards are going against you, nothing, not even counting helps. The only thing to do is leave the table. Control is the important factor.

"That's why I'm still ahead for now, Lily. When I win, I walk away quickly. Like the night we met. It's quite simple, really.

"And I know that one day when I lose too much too fast, or I'm in some masochistic payback of my own and don't leave the table fast enough, I'll fall into the quicksand which lies waiting at the end of every gambler's path. I'll become desperate, gamble for higher stakes and lose everything."

"You've become the voice of doom, Nick," I said.

"I don't want to see you fall into that black hole, Lily," he said. "You've only just crawled out of one."

"I'll keep my eyes open," I said.

"It's hard to do that when you're stoned."

"Oh piss off, Nick. I'm on a winning streak. I'll get ahead and then stop playing."

"If you can."

"I've got to take my shot."

"Of course you must, dearie." He raised my hand to his lips. The waitress opened the champagne and filled our glasses.

"Are you going to leave your husband?" he asked.

"I don't know."

I had never seriously considered the possibility that I might be the one to leave, and I knew, even as I uttered this equivocation, that I was incapable of ever taking that step. But suddenly I realized that the mere threat of my leaving was an ace in the hole I could use to bluff Paul into leaving. He could never manage the children alone, and he knew it.

"What will you do if he doesn't leave?"

"I'll go," I said.

"Good luck," Nick said, polishing off several glasses succession. He stood up, took off his jacket, stretched his lean body, his hair falling over his forehead. I caught his glance and felt a surprising flash of desire.

The power of Johnny's presence and our imminent meeting would, in the past, have precluded a strong sexual attraction for another man. Nick, as if reading my mind, sat down and touched the back of my neck lightly.

"It's difficult to believe that you were so miserable all those weeks. You look as if you could conquer the world. How did you finally get out?"

"Peasant fortitude and a taste for champagne," I said.

"I'd love some of that," he said.

"You've got good manners and Wasp wisdom instead," I said.

Nick threw back his head and laughed. His movements were slow and easy, as if he was alone. I realized that he was getting very drunk.

"You're like a ripe peach, Lily, full of juice and sweetness. What are you glowing about, woman?"

"Something happened," I said.

"Yes?"

"I ran into someone I haven't seen for a long time. We were involved and now that he's here, I'd like to see him. I'm sorry, Nick."

"No sweat, Lily, it's cool, really."

"You sound strange when you speak the language of your peers."

"And you're a bloody Italian opera, Lily."

"You say that because I'm an older woman."

"Sorry to disappoint you, Lily, but I've been with women of a certain age before. You are, however, the most excessive woman I've ever known."

"You've met me at the nadir of my life, Nick. Basically, I'm a fun-loving kid."

"That's the best part of you."

"I'm sorry about this mix-up," I said.

"It's fascinating to watch, I envy your excitement."

"Excitement can be double-edged."

"Never mind, drink your champagne and let's hit the tables. Ain't life grand?"

He motioned for the waitress and paid the check. The rock band was warming up in the stands and in the background the din of the casino was getting louder, more insistent. The overture had begun.

"I feel guilty about the way this is working out, Nick. I'd like to set the record straight. I haven't seen this man for six months. I wrote a letter ending the affair and we haven't spoken since."

"At this point my cue is to say, 'lucky bloke,' and march off into the night, but I don't want to do that. I care for you very much and I love watching your antics. But despite all of your considerable charm, there's something else."

"What?"

"It's important that I see and hear more of you."

"Why?"

"For my book."

"What do you mean, Nick?"

He stood still, looking down at me his eyes red from smoke and wine.

"I've had a lot to drink and maybe I've said too much. I hope that you won't feel inhibited now and watch every word."

"Do you mean that I'm in your novel?"

"Some things, a fleshing out of a character. During our long telephone conversations, I picked up certain things and began to use them."

"Someone once wrote that there's a splinter of ice in the heart of a writer. I feel less guilty about the weekend now."

"My generation's more casual about love affairs," he said.

"You're a gentleman to have let me off so easily."

"Is your lover a gentleman too?"

"No."

"I envy him that too."

"Being a gentleman suits you, Nick. You've even got the looks for it. Besides, you're young and too busy and ambitious to become a rat with women. That's a vocation requiring time, plotting. You have to practice your gambits for years before you can check-mate like a killer."

"Women love brutes," he said.

"*Every woman adores a Fascist,*" I quoted, "*The boot in the face, the brute brute, heart of a brute like you.*"

"Really, Lily?" he asked, wide-eyed at last.

"Sometimes," I said.

*　*　*

Walking through the casino, we approached the hundred-dollar minimum table in the baccarat pit. It was subdued. No boisterous shouts, no smiles, every one on his own. A large, powerfully built man with an air of wealth and position was playing head-to-head with the dealer. He was losing big and bad. In front of him were stacks of five hundred dollar and thousand-dollar chips. The dealer, with a lightning motion, whisked away hand after hand. The game was quick and deadly.

And still, the player did not move. He was kept at that table by a force stronger than reason or intelligence. After each whiplash of the cards, he bet his chips, each time faster than the last time. Even the dealer's mouth had begun to twitch with discomfort. Nick and I walked away just as the man began to bet his final stack of chips.

In the dim corner where Nick and I first met, a woman and a man were waiting to play. As we neared them, I saw it was Bonnie. The man with her was Marco, the young Italian who had been so deferential to Jake.

"Nick," I said, "there's Bonnie, the woman I told you about. Let's join her."

We walked over to the table.

Bonnie greeted us warmly and said that she'd called me earlier and had been told I'd left for Atlantic City. She was dressed, in contrast to her former elegance, in pants and a sweater, her bright red hair curled about her face. She looked stunning. Sid and Jake, it turned out, had left for Georgia and would be back the following night.

Marco had the elegance implicit in being young, handsome, Italian and possessed of ready cash. He gave me the requisite smoldering gaze and from his thickly waved black widow's peak to his heavy gold cuff-links, maroon satin tie and pearl-gray silk shirt, he exuded high Gucci, a priest of fashion. His jacket hugged his waist as he rose to kiss my hand, smelling faintly of vanilla. In Italy, his beauty would be commonplace, but in Atlantic City, he was Adonis.

Bonnie and I ordered markers: ten thousand for her, two thousand for me. Nick played with cash and Marco now took chips from his leather purse. Leaving the "boys" as Bonnie called them and as indeed they were, we excused ourselves and went to the ladies' room. I glanced back at the table and saw Beauty and Brains chatting away amiably. As soon as we were out of earshot, Bonnie placed her arm through mine.

"I figured you were an innocent the first time I saw you," she said.

"Hardly innocent," I said.

"Depends on where you're coming from," she said. "But since then you sure haven't let any grass grow under your feet. You're right to start with Nick. There's nothing like a young piece of ass to get the motor running again. The guys have known that for years. Has he got any money?"

"Not really. He invested everything he had in a magazine."

"No shit," she said thoughtfully, and was silent until we reached the bathroom.

Inside, we began fixing our makeup.

"You sure look great, Lily," Bonnie said, applying a thick blue pencil to her eyes. "It's not so much the dress and makeup, it's more the look of excitement in your face, all glowy. That guy Nick has sure lit your fire."

She held the eye pencil to her lips, an imaginary microphone, and sang:

> *You know that I would be a liar*
> *If I were to say to you,*
> *Girl we couldn't get much higher*
> *Come on baby, light my fire.*

She danced around playing to her image in the mirror.

"Well, Lily," Bonnie said, "that thin, pale kid must have some act. And he looks so refined. Let's all have dinner together tonight."

"I have an appointment later," I said.

"Is it the mystery man? The rat?"

"I don't want to talk about it, Bonnie."

"It must be someone special to make you look so hot. You're really off and running, Lily, nothing can stop you now."

She sat on the ledge of the sink, lit a cigarette and appraised me as I fixed my makeup. Implicit in her gaze was the knowledge that nothing would prevent me from keeping that rendezvous.

"Have a great time, babe," she said. "And talking of great times, you've got to come out to Vegas -- on a junket of course. Sid has to be there for about ten days in June and he'll be busy most of the time, so I'll be on my own. We'll hit all the funky places and have a blast. Please come, Lily."

I thought of the kids, remembering that Selena and Kitty were going backpacking right after school ended. Annie had been invited to the beach with a friend. I was free.

"Yes, I'd love to come."

"Great, now let's keep in touch this weekend. That's if your time permits, Cinderella."

We put away our lipsticks, splashed ourselves with cologne and left the bathroom arm-in-arm. "Why is Marco playing with you?" I asked, as we made our way through the long aisle of craps tables. "Doesn't he work for Jake Berman?"

"In a very informal way. Marco's a jack-of-all-trades. Sid figures I need a watchdog."

"Don't you resent that?"

"No, not really. Marco's easy to manage. I throw him some meat, he calms down and looks the other way."

"You mean..." I didn't finish the sentence.

"Yeah," Bonnie interjected quickly, "but it don't mean a thing, Lily. That's what you'll learn. Sex is just another form of barter. Anyway, Marco is nobody to throw out of bed, right?"

"What about Sid?"

"I love Sid and I'm a good wife to him. He gets what he needs from me. But I've got to have some room and I take it where and when I can get it and don't think too much about it. That's your trouble, Lily, you think too much. I can see your mind working all the time.

"You gotta start being practical. I was alone for a lot of years and I learned to take care of myself. I just hope you can do as well. It's tough -- survival of the fittest and all that jazz. Just remember, don't be too disappointed if you find yourself doing things you don't approve of. Life ain't never like it's supposed to be, babe, it's just like it is."

We rejoined Nick and Marco in time for the first shoe. They were playing two slots each, taking up the entire table. The dealer, a compact young man named Kevin, had a sense for the placement of the cards, an instinct for the swing of the deck and an inexpressive countenance. It's important to feel that the dealer is a neutral element and will spring no surprises. I had won with Kevin before.

Nick was back to double bourbons, Marco was sipping anisette and Bonnie and I drank the flat New York State champagne provided by the house. Time passed pleasantly and we were all slightly ahead when there was a sudden increase in noise and movement. The pit began to fill with people and in a few minutes the tables were full.

"Where's everyone coming from at this hour?" Nick asked.

"The last show just finished," Marco said. "I'm hungry, Bonnie, let's break for dinner."

"What time is it, Marco?" I asked.

"Twelve fifty-five," he said, glancing at his gold Rolex with a lover's eye.

"I've got to go," I said, rising.

"You've won money, Lily," Nick said, eyeing my chips. "Roughly five-hundred dollars."

"Oh?"

"Obviously you've got more important things on your mind," Nick said, "but you do lead a charmed gambler's life. You weren't even paying attention."

"OK boys, we're off to dinner," Bonnie said, gathering her chips. "I hope you'll join us, Nick."

Cramming the chips into my bag, I rose from the table and felt three sets of eyes boring into me. I walked away with as much composure as I could muster, and it wasn't until I was out of the pit and out of sight that I began to run, almost an impossibility in the crowded casino. I dodged and feinted with the precision of a halfback with a second left in a tie-score game. Sliding in and out of clusters of people, ducking to avoid lighted cigars, adrenaline coursing, all senses acute, I plunged through the crowds until I reached the deserted back hall.

I caught a glimpse of myself in the mirror, skirt flung above my knees, black-sheathed legs lifted high, hair flying, face glazed, moving forward, stretching, reaching, running for my life.

I jumped into the elevator, touching the tenth floor button. It shot up like a rocket, all systems tuned, everything easy.

Swiftly traversing the maze of corridors, I faced number eight. I took a deep breath and exhaled as the door swung open.

CHAPTER NINE

"Moonlight Becomes You" crooned Bing Crosby and I was swept into an embrace. Johnny was the spar that held me. My arms encircled his neck; my head lay in the curve of his shoulder. Moving to the music, our bodies sparked a deeper harmony, outpaced by sensation. Old adoration joined by new, we danced in a crush of memory.

Once again we had been brought together, conspirators in a dangerous exhilarating game, a powerful illicit joy. Our excitement exploded into wild laughter and we fell on the sofa still locked in each other's arms.

"If we're ever caught, there'll be no death slow enough for us," he said.

Johnny had prepared a love feast: champagne, caviar, black bread and olives.

"This should hold until later," he said, laughing and kissing me, his lips redolent of the sea.

I lit a cigarette and Johnny a cigar. Through the smoke, sipping champagne, we regarded one another silently for a long time. Johnny was naked to the waist. His face, darkened with stage makeup, contrasted strangely with the ivory tone of his body, giving him the look of a wild creature.

He never took his eyes from me, attempting to divine all that had happened in the months we'd been apart. His most salient pronouncement was in the set of his mouth which had become small and hard. Judging me, willing a revelation of my improprieties. I knew that harsh look and the question it implied: had I been quiet, unassuming, serious, moderate, virtuous? Had I carried myself correctly, conventionally, and caused no improper attentions? His wife was the model for such behavior. Yet she was not here, and had never been invited.

Long ago, I had figured out that Johnny wished me to be two women -- the exciting one he took to bed and the discreet one the world found irreproachable. He loved my body and spirit, hated my instincts and character.

Flicking a large ash from his cigar, Johnny leaned his hands on his knees and faced me.

"What the fuck are you doing here? In this zoo? Alone?" The inquisition had begun.

"I didn't know you'd be here," I stalled.

"I figured that. But that's not what I'm asking."

"Did you get my letter?"

"Yeah, I got it."

"Is that all you have to say?"

"What do you want me to say? It's words, that's all. Words don't mean a thing."

It had been a long day. I'd had too much wine, and now, after being lulled into a limpid sensuality, the thought of defending myself seemed impossible. It was, however, part of the essential nature of our bond. He imposed upon me the need to lie, yet tell the truth, to appease him and confess, to remain innocent and yet be absolved. He was sly and shrewd.

"It's hot in here," I said.

"You're wearing too many clothes," he said.

I took off my dress and leaned back on satin pillows, grateful that my rack was comfortable.

"How long has it been?" he asked.

"We haven't seen each other for six months," I said. "Since I sent you that letter."

"You shouldn't have written," he said.

"Why not?"

"It might have fallen into the wrong hands, and maybe she'd have gotten hold of it. You never know. Don't write again. Don't put anything down on paper, *ever!*"

He began pacing the floor, creating momentum for his prosecution. "And so, what are you doing here, in the fuckin' ass-end of New Jersey, on a Saturday night, looking like a two-hundred dollar hooker?"

"You're not going to like it Johnny."

"I don't like it already. I haven't liked it from the beginning. Talk!"

I wanted nothing more than to throw myself into his arms, hold him close against me and kiss him. Torn between fear and desire, I would have given anything to get him off the track of his tirade and into bed. He was intransigent. It was Italian sexual torture, an old Sicilian weapon for extracting information from the enemy. Get them down to their black lace underwear and all will be revealed. Lull them with champagne and caviar for total capitulation. He had always been a brilliant player of this game.

"Talk!"

"We're broke. My marriage is over. I'm here to win money to supplement my earnings for a couple of years. There it is, the truth, the whole truth and nothing but the truth. So help me God."

Johnny was still pacing the floor. I prayed for confrontation to be over. Just kiss me, I thought, and I'll agree to anything. I'll give you the keys to the vault, the smuggled diamonds, coded names, secret papers, microfilm and counteragents. You can have the numbered Swiss account, the jewels, and the little black book with the names sewn cleverly into my pink marabou robe. Governments will topple with the stuff I have for you. I have access to the Mossad, MI 5, the CIA. I'll swear to anything. I did it. I am Mata Hari, Elsa the Mad Bomber. I confess -- to everything, anything, but first bring your dark head close to mine and kiss me, kiss me, kiss me.

"Who's the guy?"

"What guy?"

"The one you were with in the bar and the blackjack table, the young one."

"Oh him?" I said.

"Yeah, *him*."

"How did you know I was with someone? Do you have spies?"

"Never mind, I know. I know everything," he said.

"I met him here a few months ago, long after I'd broken off with you."

Johnny's face darkened and my hopes of happiness faded.

"After it ended," I repeated. "I met him after it was over between us. I swear it was after you."

"Yeah," he said.

"There was never anyone else while I was with you."

"So you say," he said with heaviest irony, as if he were tasting the bitter gall of betrayal.

The telephone rang.

"Go ahead," I said. "Pick it up."

"It's the private line," he said, and vanished into the hall.

Grateful at first for the postponement of my trial, I became cold and restless as time passed. Finally I walked into the hall, heard his laughter and went over to the bedroom door.

Johnny was standing in the center of the room, watching himself in the mirror as he artfully smoothed back his hair, concealing his receding hairline. There was a faint, curling smile on his lips as if the picture he saw in the mirror was being projected onto the caller.

"Why, yes, my dear," he murmured into the phone, so intent upon his conversation that he didn't notice me standing a few feet away.

"I'd love to. Yes," he said, using a tone I knew well. His face glowed with pleasure at what was clearly a sexual reference. He looked young and happy. My heart strained against the onslaught of a fierce, agonizing jealousy as Johnny smiled, admiring his profile. He caught sight of me just as I turned and walked away.

I had ended the affair months ago, and what did I expect? He had never been true to me. Could I expect him to be true to my memory?

I had endured and witnessed grave suffering, but it was this jealousy that brought me to the point of madness and blind rage. I felt the stirrings of a dangerous emotion, powerful enough to unleash an act of murder. The knife quickly edged in on the smooth flesh, the flow of blood ending my anguish.

Back on the satin cushions, arms and legs flung awkwardly, I lay like a broken doll, discarded by the childish fickleness of my owner. I drank a full glass of champagne in a gulp. The phone rang and was picked up immediately. A Casanova's work is never done.

Then the bright corridors of memory flooded my mind. This is what I had renounced, never having to wonder where he was and with whom. The exquisite relief of not imagining is what I'd hoped to gain by ending our affair. Never again would I obsessively circle the dark corners of my mind; analyzing the significance of a black hair pin on a white sheet, potent as a gun, sparking a vision of black hair cascading over the bed -- his wife's or another woman's?

Once, on the phone to Johnny in Los Angeles, my ears sharp as a fruit bat, I heard the rap of high heels on the wood floor as Johnny trilled the end of a laugh. I could discern the sound of a match blown out and the deep intake of breath as he brought a cigar alive. Then, again, the rap of high heels, back and forth on the wood floor, stomping on my brain, stomping on my heart, stomping at the Savoy, stomping in Los Angeles.

"Who's there?" I had asked. His wife was not -- that I knew. "I heard high heels on the wood floor."

"You can hear the sound of heels three thousand miles away?" he said.

"I'd hear them three million miles away," I said. The sounds stopped.

"Oh," he said, "someone's here to interview me."

He threw me a lifeline and I grabbed it. But I heard the sound of those heels late into the night. Becoming a crazy passion detective, a demented female Sherlock Holmes, I gauged the height, weight and appeal of the girl in the high-heeled shoes, obsessively analyzing the clues in the latest of Johnny's crimes against love.

Johnny came back into the room and stood for a long moment in profile, head turned toward me, hands on hips, pants tightly outlining the curve of his body. He was a matador. But in lieu of bulls, he killed women. Johnny, the lady-killer.

"She just called," he said, meaning his wife. He never used first names for his wife or my husband, just he and she.

"What did she want?"

"She wanted to know if I was okay. I had a slight sore throat."

"And are you okay?"

"We'll see," he said. "So who's the young guy?"

"He's a nice kid I fucked once," I said. "Who's the girl calling on your private line at two in the morning?"

"A nice kid I fucked once," he said.

We laughed then, the tension breaking and the threads of desire winding us close again.

"What's she like?"

"Not a pain in the ass, like you. Nothing heavy, like you. Not intense, like you like it. No demands, tantrums, scenes, jealousy. No do or die, no big deal. Just a fuck.

"Have you ever been faithful to anyone?"

Instead of the quick smart retort, he looked at me over his cigar.

"For a long time there was no one but you," he said. "A very long time."

At that moment I realized for the first time, that for Johnny fidelity to a woman was a stain on his escutcheon, a betrayal of his better real self, like the loss of physical prowess or manhood.

"What's with your marriage?" he asked.

"It's over, finally."

"I've heard that before."

"It's different now."

"Why?"

"He's been very ill. I can't go on living with him; my own sanity and safety are on the line. I want my life back. It's mine and no one's going to steal it from me. No one."

"You'll be free," he said.

"That's not the point. I'm free now. I want to live."

"You've never been alone, out on your own. You're in for some big surprises. It's very cold in freedom land."

"It's pretty cold in married land, too. I'll be no more alone than I've been for years. But you're right, Johnny, I'll be free in a deeper sense. Freer than you."

He didn't look pleased at that prospect. He wanted me waiting for him, wanting only him. The balance of power had shifted.

"This is gonna make no difference in my life," he said.

"Of course not," I said. "It's got nothing to do with you."

"Don't get any ideas."

"What do you mean?"

"I'll never leave her for you," he said.

"That's the last thing I want," I said. "Do you imagine I want to be her, dealing with your temper, your women and a career that comes before everything? Alone with five kids living in friggin' Short Hills, New Jersey, seeing you when you're tired of high life and late nights. Your wife lives only through you, her surrogate tyrannical child, giving everything and getting nothing in return -- sculpting, gardening, watering the soil with tears. No thank you!"

Briefly, early in our affair I had wanted him for my own for the basest of motives, conquest and possession. However, I would have killed him at that first, inevitable betrayal. The truth was clear now. The qualities I adored in a lover would be abhorrent in a husband.

"Never fear, Johnny, I don't want to marry you. I much prefer the role of mistress."

"Smart girl. I'll tell you one thing: if we were married, there's no way we'd be in a hotel suite, half naked, drinking champagne and eating caviar at two in the morning."

"You're right, my dear. I've had your best meals and your best performances. I've even had your best years."

"All true," he said.

His capitulation complete, he rested his head against the cushions. I took his face in my hands and kissed him. He pulled me down, cradling my head in his arms, searching my face. Having learned what he wished to know, he rose abruptly, leaving me upside-down on the sofa.

"And now you're gonna support yourself by gambling? Wonderful! A real ass-hole move, *Madonna*. What are you, crazy or something?"

"There's no other way to support my family. Bills for doctors and drugs alone are staggering. I've never worked. Any job simply won't pay enough -- so I've got to win back-up money. I'm lucky at cards. I've already won thirty-thousand dollars."

"Is that enough for you?"

"It was half of what I planned to win, but Paul lost the exact amount in his last business venture. So I'm back to zero. We still have to pool our money."

"What about him?"

"He can't work now."

"Jesus, it's unbelievable! You had a fortune -- land, servants, houses, boats, cars. It can't be all gone?"

"All gone."

"What about jewelry, paintings, antiques?" he asked.

"It was sold long ago. All I have left are the furs, which are worthless. It'll be easy to spot me, selling pencils in front of Carnegie Hall. I'll be the one in the full-length sable."

"How much did he really have?"

"About twenty million."

"Jesus! And he lost it all?"

"He made it -- in a sense it was his to lose."

"You gotta have something put away."

"Paul controlled the money. It was never mine," I said. "I was treated like a child and that's the way I behaved."

"You once told me he never checked on your spending. You could've put away a bundle."

"Yes, that's true. I could have saved a fortune."

"Why didn't you?"

"It's not in my nature."

"You're on the balls of your ass now. You've got nothing."

"Not a penny. Not a sou. Nothing."

"You're incredible! What world do you live in?"

"Obviously not the right one," I said. "You'd never get into this position."

"God damn right! And now you're gonna throw yourself into that wolf pack out there. You, the dumbest broad alive. Don't you know it's a sucker's game? The only winners are the guys that own the casino. They're rich because of gamblers like you. From fuckin' believers like you. That's why I make big bucks and have suites and limos and everything I goddamn want. They pay me a fortune because of people like you!"

He paced back and forth across the room, head down. "Gamblers are losers. You're with a bunch of degenerates out there, real animals, trash. And if you go there you'll become shit like the rest of them. I've played Vegas for years, and I've seen it all. You'll be lost out there. The tables will kill you, they'll bury you alive, still screaming."

"I won't stay around long enough for that," I said. "It won't ever happen to me. I'll win and leave."

"It doesn't take long to get hooked. And don't fool yourself. That kind of high is a drug. Before you turn around, you gotta have it and then you'll turn tricks for money to play another round. You'll sell your mother to keep playing. Jesus, I don't believe it. What's happened to you?"

"I've hit bottom and I've got to get back up."

"You've certainly come to the wrong place for that."

"Tell me a better place."

"You've got kids at home."

"I'm doing this for them."

"There must be someone..."

"There's no one to give or loan us money," I said, finishing his sentence.

"But all your friends, those people you knew who were loaded -- what about them?"

"They turned their backs on Paul. He was enormously generous, with time and money -- doing incredible favors for everyone. His gentleness and kindness were legendary -- and totally forgotten. Those same people refused him when he was forced to ask for help. It was such agony for him. He was not merely refused but ignored. It broke his heart.

"Losers are like lepers," I said. "Nobody stays around when things get rough. Like the money -- all gone."

Johnny bent to retrieve some sheet music, which had fallen to the floor, arranging it with a deftness he applied to the smallest act. He turned and faced me, graceful and ferocious, a wild animal.

"I can't do anything," he said.

"I know."

"Don't put me in this position," he said. "I don't want to be having this conversation."

"You began it," I said. "But I'm not asking you for anything."

"But you will ask."

"Never."

"Just telling me that you're broke and on your ass, just letting me know is asking. Jesus, I've got my own kids and family. I can't give you anything. It's on your head if you lose."

"I never expected anything from you."

"Is there anything else you can do?"

"I could marry for money like you did. Your wife had enough so you never had to work. You could concentrate on your singing career until you made it to the big time, the big money. But never fear, my dear, it's not your money I'm after. It's your body."

"At least we both know why we're here," he said.

"Just for the record, Johnny, if you asked me for something and I had it, it would be yours, without question. For old times sake. You do know that, don't you?"

"Yeah, I know that. But it's different with me. If I gave you money, it would change everything between us. I don't want that to happen."

"No, of course not."

"Even now, on your ass, you've got the best life of anybody I know. Except me, of course."

"My life is a disaster."

"But you always manage to make everything wonderful, no matter what. You're alive and kicking, kid. You don't miss a trick."

"What do you mean?"

"Look at you! Are you having a bad time, wearing black lace underwear, eating caviar, and drinking champagne, in the most expensive suite in the hotel, with a star? Don't kid yourself, baby, you'd do anything to stay alive."

"Like you?"

"Yeah, like me. You're starting way ahead of where I began, believe me."

"How's your life been these past six months?"

"Great. Maybe I'm not quite a star yet, but soon. It's coming real soon. Everything is falling into place. I've just cut a new album and it looks terrific. We close here tomorrow night. I'll rest at home for a few days, then I've got a tour lined up for South America and a date in Vegas in June. If everything goes well, that'll be good for six weeks."

"You're leaving here tomorrow?"

"Yeah, she's coming to pick me up after the show."

I had found him only to lose him again. It would have been better not to have seen him at all. Then I remembered Bonnie's invitation.

"I'll be in Vegas in June too," I said.

"How's that?"

"I met some people last time I was here. They're arranging a junket for me, on the house, so it won't cost anything. It'll take me a few months to find a job. I'll start work when I get back."

"Who are the people?"

"Bonnie and Sid Fisher."

"I know them. Bonnie Blue was her name. I met her years ago when she was head of the chorus line at the Riviera in Vegas. I heard she married some big shot in the hotel business, right hand man to Jake Berman. Then I found out that I knew Sid too. He used to be a Hollywood agent. She was hooked on blackjack."

"Yeah. We met at a table a few months ago. She's here this weekend. We played together earlier tonight."

"She's fun, but be careful. They travel in a very fast crowd, no holds barred. Did you meet the great Jake Berman?"

"Yes."

"What did you think of him?"

"He's interesting."

"Berman's a real heavy hitter. He's very well connected and he's got his fingers into everything. You certainly got in with the right group. Did you manage to fuck Berman yet?"

"Enough!" I said. "I haven't fucked him but that doesn't mean I've ruled it out."

"If it's money you're after, Jake's certainly the man for you."

"I'm glad you approve. You know, Johnny, after all this time it's astonishing to realize how little you know me."

"I know you better than you know yourself. You don't have a clue about the things you're capable of doing out on your own. That's the part of you I do know."

"You've never believed or trusted me."

"I only know what you tell me."

"You think everyone lies and plays tricks like you. You're so evil, Johnny."

"You'd love to be me," he said.

"That's true," I said. "You lead a charmed life -- two lives, in fact. You're treated like God at home and the world adores you. You're free, handsome, rich and almost famous. And you're guilt-free."

"You were right about the things you said in your letter. They were on the mark. Yes, my dear, it was time to get up out of bed and *do* something with all that incredible energy. When I hustled, things happened real fast. My second album's going platinum in Europe."

"You've always been lucky, even when you were lazy."

"Yeah, it's true. It was perfect timing."

"You were released when you received my letter ending the affair. I'm sure you were happy to be rid of me so easily. You never called."

There was a long pause.

"The affair never ended," he said.

We looked at each other. Between us lay that question of the skin which makes all others meaningless. It had propelled me from the instant I had seen his name in lights. We rose, facing one another. Like sharks communicating through a magnetic field, we had arrived at the same place at the identical moment.

Johnny brushed his fingertips lightly across my lips, his hand moved slowly down my body and around my waist, clasping me to him in a gesture of possession. The world fell away, spinning us into the scintillating sphere of a brilliant sensuality, an orbit of desired light.

We lay in the sun of our passion. It grew bright and hot, burnishing our skin, heating the blood, deepening desire. Then the moon eclipsed the sun and there were darker pleasures, every intimacy thrusting us farther into a primitive past. We had been dinosaurs together, and like dinosaurs, we would in the end have devoured one another.

And then the other, became the one. The next rapture was beyond time. We lay still, in our little death. Hands, lips, bodies welded in the heat of love, the last frame of a living ecstasy.

CHAPTER TEN

I awoke chilled. Johnny lay on the far end of the bed. Moving close to him, I basked in the warmth of his sleeping body.

We had made love until dawn and although it was still quite early, I was restless, anxious to return to my room, not wanting to linger and rouse quiescent yearnings. I'd suffered them too often.

I remembered another time. Lying in a hotel bed, still warm with love, and Johnny leaping out of bed into the shower, dressing in seconds. The harsh brush of his tweed jacket scratched as he kissed me good-bye, hair damp and eyes averted. The door slammed shut like a slap. It's always easier to be the first to leave.

"She'll be here early afternoon," he said, waking as I kissed him. "Don't call, I'll be in touch. Take care, baby."

During the hours I'd been with him, he hadn't once used my name. Had he ever? Was I just another anonymous "she"? And in the recesses of his heart, how did he name me?

Returning to my room, I was relieved there were no messages. I lay on the bed and fell into a deep sleep, waking with all my suppressed longings. A night of love intensifies the desire for passion. I felt deeply lonely.

*   *   *

I called Nick's room just as he was about to leave for breakfast and pressed him to wait for me. I dressed quickly and met him in the lobby.

Atlantic City's incredible decay was startling in the light of morning. It was a slum-near-the-sea: cracked pavements, filthy streets, rows of collapsed tenements, revealing the rot beneath everything.

We entered a diner called Hoagie Heaven and the juke box was playing James Taylor's "You've Got a Friend. "The employees were straight out of a thirties movie: the waitress, a slattern with a sulky smile, waiting for a lucky break, the unctuous, mustachioed proprietor, the temperamental Oriental cook who shouted continuously.

The cuisine was a taste of childhood's forbidden pleasures -- greasy, messy and much. The texture of white bread and starch covered everything: sticky buns, stacks of french fries glistening with oil, hero sandwiches thick with sausage and onions, drippy, buttered toast, runny pies and chicken-fried steak.

Nick, miserable and ravaged, was in no mood to speak. We ate ravenously: eggs, bacon, pancakes and spaghetti with dark brown sauce washed down with cups of hot, metallic coffee and blueberry pie a la mode. I was in a state of hunger and crippling fatigue brought about by gambling, drugs, champagne and making love to excess. We sat smoking and drinking coffee, staring out at the pathetic squalor of the street.

"Time to gamble," Nick said, in a voice hoarse with drink and smoke. "Let's go to the bar. I need a drink before hitting the tables."

We sat at the same table as the previous night. The bar seemed shabby now, empty except for a few tapped out gamblers. They looked shocked, as if they'd just received tragic news and had to anesthetize themselves with drink before counting their losses.

Nick ordered a double bourbon. His silent brooding had further lowered my spirits. The exuberant optimism and excitement of the previous evening was gone. He took off his dark glasses and looked at me with red, shrunken eyes.

"What on earth happened to you last night?" I asked, finally.

"Everything," he said. "I stayed too long at the fair. So much for being smart and knowing the rules of the game."

He took my hand and placed it on his hot brow and closed his eyes. "Your hand feels so cool," he said. "Let it rest there for a moment."

"You look ready to drop, Nick. Have you slept?"

"Not much," he said. "Oh, Lily, I've done a terrible thing."

"Stop drinking. It'll only depress you further. You need a cold shower."

"That's the first time I've ever heard you sound like a mother."

"Did you imagine that I was an impostor, an adventurer posing as a mother of three daughters?"

"I think that you're both mother and impostor," he said.

"It's a beautiful day, let's go out on the boardwalk. The fresh air will clear your head. All the recycled air in the casino and the bourbon are killing your brain cells."

"I'd be happy just to get through the next hour," he said, holding my hand tightly. I sensed then, the maternal love he'd never known: cool fingers on his brow, the passionate attachment of blood, and all the tender, mother-ministering privileges of childhood.

We walked out into a windy March day, bright with sunshine and shimmering with sand and sea. Everything sparkled and glowed. After days in the casino, it was like seeing the world for the first time. The ocean gleamed, spinning foam and filling the air with the smell of the sea.

We took a long walk, eventually turning into a coffee shop near the hotel.

Beating a spoon nervously against the Formica tabletop, Nick began to speak, his eyes wandering uneasily around the room.

"My magazine sent off a lot of sparks. Publishers and agents have been impressed. Writers have been contracted for books and articles. The literary community has really begun to respond."

He paused, pained, his boyish face revealing strains and fears that were usually masked by an expression of impassive, calm confidence.

"My father was a talented writer who never had the chance to fulfill his gift because of family commitments. I wanted somehow to justify his life with his money.

"My mother died of pneumonia when I was about a year old. After her death my father drank heavily and died just a few years later of a damaged liver. Jesus, I tell a lousy story."

He stared out the window glassily and then brought a hand to his eyes. "It's not only the magazine, but the staff will suffer," he said. "They've existed on minimum salary, working twenty hours a day, and if I can't repay the loan I took out and run the magazine for a few months longer, then everything's gone. Time and an energetic, viable literary reality. The money that I'll lose personally is the least of it."

Pausing again, he took a deep breath as if suddenly winded.

"I came down here this weekend to win enough to repay what I'd borrowed," he said, catching my eyes and holding them. "I lost fifty-thousand dollars last night."

"My God," I said.

"Twenty-thousand in cash and thirty-thousand in markers. The only thing I've got left is ten-thousand in credit."

"What are you going to do?"

"I've got two choices. I can leave immediately and scrounge around for the money, or at least part of it. That seems an impossible task since I have no collateral and have used all my borrowing power. The second option, of course, is to use the ten-thousand to win back fifty-thousand."

Engaging in this conversation directly outside a casino was ridiculous. Given the situation and the place, there could be no doubt about what he would do, and in fact had already started doing.

"Let's gamble," he said. This interval filled with confessions and self-laceration had been only a prelude to the madness, a time to measure the losses and review expectations. "So much for card-counting and the idea that I was in command," Nick said.

There was a tremor to the hand that held the coffee mug and the fingernails were bitten raw. He was utterly transformed from the self-confident, urbane young man with whom I'd drunk champagne in celebration less than twenty-four hours ago.

"At least now you don't have to envy me," I said. "You're out on your own edge now. You've made that leap into the absurd. From the ramparts of Newport to the swamps of New Jersey in one fell swoop."

"That's just what I seem to have done," Nick said. "In some awful way, it's exhilarating."

"More frightening than exhilarating," I said.

"I'm going to use the ten-thousand to win fifty," he said.

"Of course you are. I never doubted that you would. Consider yourself the recipient of the Kierkegaard Fear and Trembling Award and the Sartre-Camus prize for the best existential ploy of a budding novelist. The ultimate out-on-a-limb move."

"And where are you after last night, Lily? Farther out on your particular limb?"

"Of course," I said. "But I'm too concerned with real problems to permit myself the luxury of caring, or considering the consequences of last night. I need a miracle, and quickly."

"How much of a miracle?"

"Enough for two years of living expenses, about sixty-thousand dollars."

"What about your husband?"

"He's my responsibility, if he needs me."

"I don't understand."

"In sickness and in health," I said.

"You really feel that way?"

"Yes.

"Yet you want a separation?"

"Absolutely."

"That's a contradiction, Lily."

"Feelings don't vanish because it's inconvenient to have them, Nick. There are certain loyalties and bonds that *are* indissoluble. We grew up together, we had three children and were everything to one another for a long time."

I'd begun to cry. Nick reached over and touched my arm across the table. I pulled away, fearful that his comfort would burst the dam of my sorrow and drown us.

"You must love him very much," Nick said.

"I will love him always."

"It's too complicated for me."

"I don't understand it either."

* * *

The Saturday afternoon casino was filled with crowds lining up for the slots, holding their cups like mendicants. We pushed through the throng and separated at the blackjack games.

Reluctant to play now, I walked through the casino trying to recover from Nick's shocking news. I resolved to play carefully, building slowly and getting ahead before pressing my bets. This meant that I'd have to stay in Atlantic City beyond the weekend.

Watching a high-limit game for a while, I looked up and saw Bonnie and Marco immaculate in white flannels and sweaters, looking like an ad for lawn tennis.

"Ah, the prisoner of love," she said in a low voice, kissing my cheek.

Marco kissed my hand, bestowing a connoisseur's glance to ascertain the exertions and pleasures of the previous night.

"Are you winning?" Bonnie asked.

"I haven't played yet, it's too crowded. The only seats are at the hundred-dollar table."

"I'm dying to play," Bonnie said. "I never got back down to the casino last night. We ate and drank until I was too tired. I like your friend Nick, he seems fascinated by you. And speaking of admirers, Jake will be here tomorrow. I just spoke to him and Sid on the phone and he wanted to know if you'd still be here. How long are you staying?"

"A few more days."

"That's great."

"I don't know that I'm interested in Jake, Bonnie. I've got enough to keep me busy for the next few days."

"Be smart, Lily," she said. "Jake's the kind of guy that you want in your corner."

Bonnie and I slid into two seats that opened at a twenty-five dollar table and Marco left for baccarat.

My hands shook as I placed five hundred dollars in chips on the green felt. Lighting a cigarette in an attempt to control a mounting panic, I closed my eyes and immediately the terror was revealed. It was there, always, in the deepest recesses of my heart. I saw Paul at home, alone, sick and frightened and felt his pain and the constant anxiety that tormented the children.

Suddenly everything closed in on me: the dealer's impassivity, the din, the stacks of chips, the drinks and the smoke. My desperation crested. I wanted to scream: "Enough! Let me out! Make him well and give me peace and I'll trade anything, years of life and future happiness. Only let this torment pass."

A wave of depression washed over me, pulling me under, drowning me, and then Johnny's face -- smiling, captivating, beckoning. I saw myself running toward him the previous night, hoping for a miracle of love to sustain my spirit. I'd found varied pleasures and pains, escape and the evanescent warmth of animal excitement. But there hadn't been, even for a small moment, the tender empathy that I'd yearned for, almost more than all the rest.

"What's the matter, Lily? You look strange?" Bonnie asked.

"I'm scared."

"That's no way to play. Come with me."

After reserving our seats, I followed Bonnie through the hotel and up to her suite. She locked the door, left the room and returned with a jar of white powder and two tiny silver spoons.

"Instead of Dutch courage, I give you Peruvian power," she said.

"That's just what I need, power."

"I know the signs well. Anyway, you're an easy read, Lily. Never play poker, honey, everything you feel is written all over your face. What happened last night to make you feel so terrible?"

"It left me exactly where I knew it would, although I wished for something more. Everything has accelerated now, including my desperation. I'm afraid I've used up my luck."

"You've got luck coming your way, you're lucky, period. I'm a good judge. I've spent so many years in casinos. I could set up shop as a fortune teller."

"I hope you're right, Bonnie."

"Gamblers know the look, you've got it."

She went to the bar and poured us Dubonnet and soda.

"You've got other assets too, Lily. You just haven't figured out how to use them. Sit back, relax. We'll work out a plan of action. What's your bankroll at this point and how much do you need to win?"

"I've got a credit line of thirty-thousand dollars," I said.

"I'm not talking credit. I'm asking what you've got to risk, the amount you can to pay back if you lose?"

"Nothing. It's the truth but nobody seems to believe me."

"It's unbelievable, considering you were so rich."

"I've got the five-hundred I won last night. I could lay my hands on the thirty thousand for a few days. It's in my name but now that Paul's lost that amount, it's going for rent, food, school and a stack of medical bills. Paul has the rest, but it's not much."

"Jesus, no wonder you're scared."

"And I've got to win it quickly. Most of it at least, over the next few days."

"And I thought I had balls!" Bonnie said.

"I just hope my nerve holds out."

"You're in deep shit, Lily. I've been hooked on blackjack for years but basically I know I'm covered, one way or the other. And what I don't have covered, I can always get somewhere."

She smiled enigmatically and rose to freshen our drinks.

"The guy that you were with last night, is he the same one you told me about the first time I met you?"

"Yes."

"Ask him for money."

"He's made it clear it's out of the question."

"You had an affair with him for three years, he's rich and you can't ask him for anything?"

"That's it."

"He must be some winner," she said.

"He doesn't want the responsibility, the emotional bond that giving money implies."

"Bullshit, Lily. He's just a cheap, selfish bastard."

"He doesn't owe me anything, Bonnie."

"That's beside the point. He must know about your financial problems, your husband's illness. He's got to see you're crazy with fear. He doesn't have to give you big bucks necessarily, although what's wrong with that if he's loaded? I just mean for him to give you a little to fall back on, a couple of thousand, expenses, a loan, just something to ease the strain. It helps to know someone cares. I know how much the gesture itself means. Did he offer to give you anything at all?"

"He warned me they'd kill me out on the tables."

"And he's willing to let you be killed?"

"I don't belong to him, I'm not his responsibility."

"He certainly used you as if you belonged to him," she said. "A three-year affair is no casual fling."

"I used him. For warmth, for the image of myself that he gave me, for excitement and escape. He helped me to stay alive all these years."

"No one can do that for anyone else. You kept yourself alive."

"He's an extraordinary lover," I said.

"That's another story, Lily. I understand that hook too. But never forget, honey, that you're one-half of that fabulous dance team."

Bonnie slid the jar of cocaine toward me. "You're just a beginner. Wait till you're really free. There's a lot of great sex out there. What you think is number one now, will just be where you begin when you really start to ball. Life's changed, Lily."

I hadn't done coke for several months and the high was swift. Layers of fatigue and pain sloughed off like dead skin. In minutes I was fresh, hopeful and ebullient.

"Here's coke for later," Bonnie said, handing me a miniature vial. "You'll need this if you've got to win a lot of money fast."

Bonnie, having done several lines of coke, was now laughing at what had seemed tragic a few moments ago.

"What are going to do after you win the money, champ?" she asked.

"I'm going to find a job."

"You sure got a lot going for yourself. There's nothing like starting out late and poor. But never fear, Lily, Jake will be here tomorrow. There's a garden you should cultivate, it's where the green stuff grows. He could help you, and he's very generous to those he likes, especially women."

"That's not my style, Bonnie."

"Time to change. The style you've got now doesn't seem to be doing wonders for you."

After a couple of lines of coke, we drifted out of the suite infinitely gayer than when we'd entered. Believing that magic engenders magic, I could scarcely wait to play. I was anticipating what I'd feared just moments before.

When we got back to the table, I glanced over at Nick. His continued presence augured well: he was still in the game.

I ordered a marker and laid five black hundred-dollar chips on the green felt, signaling for change. However, just as the dealer reached for the chips, I pulled them back. Then I put a black hundred-dollar chip in the betting slot.

The cocaine had placed me on the keen edge of excitement. Encapsulated in the brilliance and force of the black chip the cards flew into place, I caught a red King and a black Ace. Blackjack!

It had all the punch and power of love at first sight. The dealer, however, had an ominous ace showing. I declined his offer of insurance, which would have given me even money, a discreet and sensible move. I wanted all or nothing. He flipped over his hole card. It was a nine. I'd won a hundred and fifty dollars.

I bet the entire two hundred-fifty and received a three and a seven. I doubled-down against the dealer's nine and pulled the optimum card, an ace, an ace, giving me a twenty-one. Ahead a thousand dollars by the third round, I was now betting with five hundred dollar chips.

My heart lurched wildly as I was dealt two threes. The dealer had a five showing. The indicated play was to split the threes, which meant putting up another five hundred dollars. I moved a purple chip next to the first and prayed for a swift release. I was instead dealt a seven on one three, calling for another double down.

At that moment my marker arrived. I bet another five hundred again, got a neat ten, making a total of twenty -- so far, so good. The remaining three received an ace, still another double-down bet. I got a six, making another twenty. The next thing I heard was a cheer. The dealer busted. I was ahead three thousand dollars in three hands.

Electric currents of excitement shot through me. My pulse roared in my ears and the blood rushed to my head, flaming my face. All I could hear was the ragged, rough sound of my own breathing. My consciousness narrowed to eyes and hands, moving the chips swiftly, surely, over the cards, fingers flying, guided by an impetus surer than judgment, swifter than impulse. I was in the grip of an emotion as strong as any I'd ever known. The excitement became unbearable, blinding me so that I could no longer see the cards. But I knew above all, that I was pushing hard and winning big. Chips were doubled, tripled, and flung everywhere -- no neat piles now, just racing in the teeth of the wind, faster and faster, escalating my bets into the thousands on each hand.

I was on a streak and met and paced its mad course with an instinctive rhythm -- trusting it, spurring it, using it until I could again see everything before me: optimum cards, miraculous draws, winning hands, all the panoply of pure luck, powerful and prodigious, lavish and limitless.

It was a dream of beneficence, every wish granted, magically fallen into place. All those inchoate yearnings of childhood fulfilled, the revelation of my true heart, the hoped for recognition, the love of the Gods, the marriage of true minds, the power and the glory of perpetual hope realized. At last.

CHAPTER ELEVEN

"You did it baby, you beat 'em," Bonnie said.

"<u>Brava</u>, <u>bravissima</u>," said Marco, kissing me on both cheeks.

"Bless you my dear," said Nick, hugging me. "I saw you from across the room and even from that distance I knew that you were winning. It was like watching a great horse come in at the finish line. Everyone in the pit was rooting for you."

"Let's get out of here and up to my suite for a glass of champagne. You look as if you're ready to faint," Bonnie said.

I was given a rack for the chips and went to the back counter of the cashier's window. Marco removed, stacked and sorted the chips expertly, counting and restacking them several times, his fingers graceful and sure.

"Thirty-eight-thousand dollars," he said. Marco had probably begun his career as a dealer.

The cashier recounted the chips, subtracted my marker for twenty-five hundred dollars and gave me a check for thirty-five thousand dollars. I took five hundred in cash and placed the check in the safety deposit box. When we reached Bonnie's suite I collapsed on the bed.

"You'll feel better soon," Marco said.

"I can't stop trembling."

"You were high on coke and the winning streak shot you over the top," Bonnie said. "You're shaky, Lily. You'll be fine after a little rest."

Covering me with a blanket, she propped me up with pillows, brought me orange juice and a cold cloth for my head while Marco massaged my feet. They'd obviously been through these rites before. Finally, they left me to rest in the darkened room. After about twenty minutes I called Paul, bracing myself for disaster.

"Hello," he said.

"How do you feel?"

"I'm better. Finally, the pills are working. Also I had some good news today."

"What?"

"A small stroke of luck. Two years ago, my lawyer instituted a suit on my behalf against some builders who'd reneged on a contract. They've decided to settle out of court and he accepted a deal for me."

"How much?"

"It's not a lump sum, I'm afraid. The money's to be paid out in notes over a period of two years. The full amount is thirty-thousand, but in order to get the money sooner, the notes have to be discounted and Harry has to be paid. The net amount will be reduced to about twenty-thousand."

"It's a good omen," I said.

"I hope so, Lily. It's a relief to have something coming in after such a long, dry spell. The first installment of five thousand will be coming through in a few months. And we need it."

"Are things that bad?"

"Yes. The money you won went to pay a load of bills, some almost six months old. Now we've got three months of due bills. We're almost down to the wire."

Suddenly I was imbued with a familiar sense of being one with Paul, of striving for the same goals.

"I've got another surprise for you Lily," he said.

"What?"

"I'm leaving."

"What do you mean?"

"I'm moving out. Separating."

"Really?"

"Yes. There's a larger apartment available in my office building. I've spoken to the landlord and he'll adjust the prepayment on the old apartment so that the new rent's nominal. I'll have a combined living and working space, a perfect arrangement for me."

"All of those prepayments to your accountant, lawyer, insurance and rent have saved out lives."

"I think I planned it that way unconsciously."

"When are you leaving?"

"In about four weeks."

"So soon."

"It's what you wanted, Lily."

"A new life," I said.

I was stunned at Paul's news, and by the sense of unity between us that his imminent departure had created. His decision seemed arbitrary and unreal, rather than like something I'd been struggling for years to attain.

"The old life has the history and memory of too many failures, " Paul said. "It was crazy of me to suggest that you leave. There's no way I could ever manage to run the apartment and the children's complicated lives. Annie's schedule alone proved too taxing for me to cope with for even a few days. I can barely handle myself. There's no way I would've forced you to leave your home."

"You certainly sounded as if you would. You threatened me."

"You must forgive me, Lily. I lost control. I never meant any of it. I hate myself more for the way I've treated you than you can ever imagine.

"The time has come to release you from the burden of taking care of me. You have to work now, it's essential and you'll need your energy for other things."

"I'm going to look for a job as soon as I get back."

"I owe you a great deal. If our roles had been reversed, I couldn't have done this for you."

"We do what we can."

"And for the violence..." His voice broke. "Forgive me. I can't express how ashamed and guilty I feel."

"Forget it, it's over." I said, quickly.

"How are you doing at the tables?" he asked.

"I won thirty-six-thousand dollars," I said.

"That's great! Now get out of there fast, Lily, before you piss it all away."

"Don't tell me what to do," I said. "I won it, it's mine."

Rejoining the others, I found Nick lying on the couch, eating grapes and drinking champagne.

"I'm free," I said. "Paul's leaving in two weeks. He has an apartment and there's been an unexpected turn of fortune, money from an old law suit."

"What a prodigiously lucky day for you, Lily. You've won a new life," Nick said.

"And thirty-six-thousand dollars." said Marco.

"And in one shoe," Bonnie said. "All your wishes have come true, Lily. I told you that you're lucky and I was right."

"An ordinary life," I said. "Ordinary despairs."

Bonnie rose, champagne held aloft. "To Lily." she said, and they all clinked glasses.

"And now it's time for me to get back to the casino. They seem to be giving money away down there. I've got to make hay while the sun shines. Sid will be here in a few hours."

The others left with her and I returned to my room. The phone rang as I entered. It was Johnny.

"Did you just call several times and hang up?" he asked.

"No," I said. "You told me she was arriving early. It must have been one of your groupies."

"I can't fuckin' sleep now that the phone got me up," he said.

"Have the switchboard hold your calls. That's if you can bear to postpone hearing from today's fresh batch of victims."

Johnny snorted a laugh.

"Yeah, yeah. So what's happening with you?"

"Paul's leaving in a month. We're separating at last."

"That *is* news. What happened?"

"He's found a place to live. And he's got some money coming in."

"You don't sound thrilled."

"I'm tired."

"How'd you do at the tables?"

"I won thirty-six-thousand dollars."

"Time to go home."

"Where I'm supposed to wait patiently for your phone call if you can see me for a few hours?"

"You'd be a fool not to wait for that call. It doesn't get any better than last night."

The doorbell rang, and he hung up. I knew that Johnny was upset by Paul's leaving. My freedom placed him at a disadvantage, changing the balance of our relationship. Now it was his turn to wonder where I was and with whom.

The phone rang again. It was Nick, anxious to come up and talk. He was at the door in minutes and swept into the room.

"I won twenty-thousand dollars," he said, "but I simply can't go back into the casino and do battle again, Lily. I've got to take the thirty-thousand loss."

"Take the money and run," I said.

"I'll cover my losses by selling some family things that were left to me. I'll trade my car for a cheap wreck, live frugally and write fast. When the book's published, I'll make some money."

"Need is a great form of inspiration."

"I'm going to leave right now, Lily."

"Of course. Don't worry about me, I'm fine."

"We both know that if I stay, I'll be back at the tables. I hope you understand."

"Don't worry about me. I'm fine."

"If you come with me, I'll drop you off in New York."

"Oh God, not you, too! Everyone's telling me to leave. I really can make that decision myself."

Nick grabbed me and hugged me to him. "Are you still my Madame Bovary?" he asked.

"We're past that, I'm free now, so we'll have to use another script. Besides, she came to a bad end and I have other plans for myself."

"Come up to Boston for a sexy weekend. Plenty of chocolate ice-cream and champagne."

"What lady could refuse an offer like that? Certainly not me."

"We'll be friends, always?"

"Of course. We knew that from the very beginning. Friends at the very least, but maybe, after all, the very most."

We said good-bye and just before he left, a wave of longing struck us, and we kissed.

Nick's departure set me further adrift. I had drawn strength and a sense of renewal from his youth. And implicit in every relationship between a man and a woman, no matter how disparate their lives, there exists the possibility of true union. That tropism toward the other, the male, was as inbred in me as the color of my eyes.

*　　*　　*

A buzzer rang and the bellman presented me with a jungle of orchids. The card:

Please join me for dinner. My suite, ten-thirty. Jake.

It was less an invitation than a command, tempered only slightly by the tender of expensive flora. I remembered Jake's extraordinary blue eyes and the iron will that lay beneath his controlled exterior. I'd wondered at his persistence in keeping in touch. It couldn't be for things that he had surfeit of in Las Vegas: youth, beauty and easy availability. He had an enormously busy, glamorous life and yet somehow there was something he wanted from me.

I dressed quickly, which allowed me an hour and a half in the casino before dinner. The work of the day finished, it was pleasant to play mindlessly, having no greater stake than an hour's amusement.

Although I had looked forward to seeing Jake, once the power of the game began, I preferred to remain absorbed in fantasy, recapturing the absolute wonder of childhood. Then, the greatest games were the secret ones. While skating or jumping rope or playing hopscotch, I subdued evil, conquered lands, won battles, received prizes, merited tributes and exacted accolades. In my imagination, reality was refashioned and I was made master of my world.

Playing at center seat, a sharp-looking man in an expensive suit was anchor. First-base was manned by an over-bearing woman in her sixties wearing a loud print dress and rhinestones. She repeatedly threatened the dealer with dire punishment if she did not get good cards. Another player, puny and unshaven, nervously jiggled change in his baggy pants as he engaged in a running commentary with the cards. He seemed to be trying to talk his way to luck, the way a cheerleader raises the spirits of the team.

All gamblers seek an intimation of destiny. In a world where we are all at the mercy of fate, it is gambling, strangely enough, which provides for many an illusion of control. There is the sense that a shout into the void will elicit a response, if only for an instant. High in the pantheon of classic escapes, gambling can be as addictive and powerful as drugs, alcohol and sex. From the alleyways of ancient Samothrace to the luxurious gaming palaces of the Riviera to Wall Street, its universal appeal has been proven again and again.

The epic swings of my own destiny met and matched the violent reversal of fortune in the casino. I was accustomed to the drama of Paul's rapid rise to wealth and the feverish anxiety of his fall. Although I had abhorred and feared his ruthless aggression, another part of me had always envied the excitement and power of his business life. All those years I had lived through Paul, sharing his adventures and the luxuries, which they provided. I had chosen him, in part, because I yearned to possess his energy and courage. And when I'd begun to gamble, I had, like Paul, everything to win and nothing to lose.

A casino is like great theater. It stages a perpetual morality play with alternating characters, the submissive groveling player, begging the dealer for mercy, the flirtatious woman, currying favor by sexual innuendo, the angry, abusive player, the silent stoic, the cajoler promising the dealer rewards, the devout player, tipping to insure victory, the cool and silent professional, the hot and sweaty amateur.

There are gamblers who, like actors desperate for an audience, solicit attention from their tablemates, creating little scenes and melodramas. There are those timid, lonely souls who gamble to create a social life, having only the dubious companions of the casino for friends. And there are the elderly retirees for whom a trip to the casino is a day's outing with their peers, a chance to absorb life and watch the action.

Happy now to take a bit part in the evening's drama, I played on, absorbed in the repetitive movements of the dealer, content to watch the cards slide by, relieved that I was no longer trembling.

"*Ciao, bella,*" said a voice near me. It was the redoubtable Marco, shaking his head in comic disbelief.

"You won this afternoon, *cara,* and still you play?"

"I played for money then. This is for pleasure."

"So tell me, how much have you lost for pleasure?"

I looked at the chips and was surprised to see how many were gone.

"I've lost five-hundred dollars."

"Stop now, cara, your luck has turned. Jake asked me to find you, he's free now."

"I can't stop playing yet. I've got to win back my five-hundred dollars."

"You can play again, tomorrow or later."

He said nothing more, standing quietly behind me as I continued to lose.

"I'm stuck eight-hundred dollars. I can't leave!"

"Be lucky," he said.

Alternating twenty-five and fifty-dollar bets, I won splits and doubles on the fifty-dollar bets and by the end of one shoe I had won back most of my money. At that point I was relieved to leave with Marco. What had begun as amusement had rapidly become fraught with anxiety. It would have been no fun at all to lose a thousand dollars.

"You're lucky, Lily," Marco said, "But you must learn to use your head. It's like car racing. If you race enough times the odds are that you'll crash and hurt yourself badly or die, no matter how many races you won before."

He turned the full force of his amorous smile upon me. It had no ulterior meaning. It was simply his instinctive reaction to being with a woman. His hand, positioned at the small of my back, guided me through the casino.

In the elevator, I had a moment of acute panic and disorientation. It was bizarre to have dinner with a man whom I scarcely knew, merely because he had requested my presence. Bonnie had succeeded in stimulating my curiosity about Jake, but I could barely remember him. His strange persistence, the proposed trip to Vegas and Bonnie's talk of his power had placed me in this position, I would have preferred to play blackjack at a five-dollar table and eat chili on the windy boardwalk.

The door was opened by a manservant who took my jacket and offered me champagne. Marco disappeared into an adjoining room.

The suite, stripped of conventional hotel furniture had been transformed into an English study: dark wood paneling and floors, antique Persian carpets and Queen Anne furniture. A poetic landscape illuminated by a small light hung over the Adam mantel. The windows were covered with blue velvet drapes. The bookcases lining the walls were filled with leather-bound editions. I was reminded of the morning I'd awakened to an apartment totally altered.

The contrast to the rest of the hotel was astonishing. I would not have been surprised to see Jake enter in a red jacket, dressed for the hunt. He arrived, instead, wearing jeans, a checkered shirt and sneakers, looking older and more worn than when I'd last seen him.

Although he greeted me warmly, the first moments were awkward and strained. The presence of Bonnie or even Marco would have made it easier. Having begun on a bad note, my usual volubility was silenced. The absurdity of the situation was exacerbated by the strangeness of being in an English study, above a casino, in a hotel in Atlantic City. Having no sense of where I was or with whom, I felt a very old Alice indeed.

"I'm happy you've come, Lily," he said.

"This is a beautiful room," I said.

"I'm here often and I prefer to have my own things," he said. "Bonnie tells me you had a big win this afternoon."

"It's been a day of momentous changes. Has Bonnie told you the rest?"

"You've separated from your husband."

"You're up on all the news."

"How do you feel?"

"It's something I've wanted for a long time. I feel ambivalent but basically relieved."

"Have you seen a lawyer?"

"No."

"Are you financially protected?"

"Protected from whom and by what?"

"I'm referring, of course, to the assets, money and property."

"My winnings of this afternoon are the assets. The apartment is a rental and everything that could've been sold is gone. There are stacks of back bills."

"Really?" He looked at me as if I'd made a bad joke.

"Hasn't Bonnie filled you in on that yet?"

"She told me your husband ran into some bad luck, started with nothing, made a fortune, then lost it. What does he do now?"

"He's depressed and unable to work."

"That's sad. Tragic."

Jake's simple, humane response set me at ease at once. There was a great relief in being understood and his sympathy touched me.

"Every man who's ever made a fortune by his own wits has gambled for very high stakes and there's always a down-side risk in that. From what Bonnie tells me, that's what happened to your husband."

"He'd gotten used to betting and winning -- he never thought he'd lose, ever."

"I started from nothing too, and I know very well that to make it big, alone, is an incredible accomplishment. Make no mistake business is a jungle. To get to the top requires an amazing combination of courage, endurance and luck. It's a long, painful fall down that mountain. Few men could withstand the crash.

"You'd better watch out, Lily, you're gambling too. The only difference is that the financial world was his craps' table."

"Of course that's occurred to me," I said. "But my aims are different. I'll stop soon."

"Just remember that you're in a different position from when you started out. You had nothing to lose then. Now you're ahead thirty-five thousand. You've got to support and raise your kids, without a father in residence. That's very tough stuff for a woman like you."

Our dinner was brought by a small platoon of waiters who set up a table with white linen, fresh flowers and sparkling crystal and china. We were served by the butler. Nothing works up a thirst like discussing imminent poverty in an atmosphere of luxury.

We dined leisurely on oysters, wild duck and chocolate mousse. I ate and drank with the abandon usually reserved for post-funereal feasts. We talked of our families. Jake's three children were scattered over the country, and although not estranged, they rarely saw one another. The subject of his first wife still absorbed him and he was grateful to have a chance to talk about her. It was evident that he'd never recovered from her loss.

"We were childhood sweethearts," he said. "She was with me from the very beginning. You can never replace that history with anyone else. We'd just finished having the ranch built when she was killed."

"I'm sorry," I said.

"People don't like to talk of the dead, it makes them uncomfortable. But when I talk about what we had together, I feel close to her again. We came a long way together from the streets of Williamsburg."

"Brooklyn?"

"Yes," he said.

"That's where I grew up," I said.

Jake's face broke out into a smile I'd never seen.

"That explains it," he said, rising, "why you're so familiar to me, as if I'd known you before! Williamsburg -- that's it! You're just a kid from Brooklyn."

After that, we were like long-lost friends. Although Jake had been there twenty-five years before I had, our visions of the old neighborhood matched, both lit by a soft nostalgic glow. We had attended the same schools and fondly remembered all the same landmarks: lover's lanes, ice-cream parlors, pizza joints, delis, movie theaters, and the library. We'd even shared two distinguished English teachers.

"I couldn't stop thinking about you, Lily. There was something about you. At first, I thought it was because you reminded me of my wife. And that's true, too. But it was also the Brooklyn that I saw in you, the Brooklyn that made you familiar to me. You had qualities I recognized instinctively."

Jake selected a long Havana cigar from an ebony and silver humidor.

"Strange as it sounds, Lily, I must've seen myself in you, things that reminded me of my early years. Growing up, working around the clock, going to school at night, sleeping in a corner of the living room, everybody struggling. Individuality was treasured, fostered. All the guys had their nicknames. Everyone was a character. Craziness was celebrity. When I met you, I told you that you were an anomaly, an old-fashioned girl in a world of liberated women."

"I'm hardly old-fashioned."

"Maybe more than you think. I've been around the block a couple of times and you're an odd combination. You've lived one kind of life, programmed to be wife and mother, and now you've been pushed out of your groove. You would've remained there forever if circumstances hadn't forced you out of the house. It'll be interesting to see what becomes of you and what you make of yourself."

"My first priority is financial independence."

"You'll have to be tough and independent in every way. You're really just starting out now. If you want it enough, it'll come to you. I've always had great faith in will power, in tenacity and determination. I was catapulted out of my comfortable life when my wife died. She was my world, and I always thought she'd be there with me.

"Business became my life then. I put everything into that and I became more successful than I'd imagined. But I have a hard time being close to a woman. I can't seem to replace my wife in any way. We needed no one but each other, not even children.

"I have access to other lives and great mobility. There are the social and business scenes here and in Europe, but I don't feel comfortable with those people. I'm just a Brooklyn boy at heart."

"I can't imagine that you have the time to be lonely," I said. "You're life's full, fascinating and you love your work."

"I'm addicted to work and of course I've got my art collection. I'm afraid that it takes the place of a personal life. There's that too, you'll have to face, Lily. Being alone."

"You can be alone even when you live with someone."

"But the real thing is different, Lily. You'll have to reinvent yourself."

"My choices aren't vast, Jake. I'm going to try to get a job reading scripts, editing, or doing public relations. I'm not really sure. It depends on where I can make the most money and rise the quickest. I've never had a job."

"Whatever the odds, Lily, don't sell yourself short. You're ambitious, more than you imagine. When are you coming to Vegas?"

"Early June. It'll be my last gambling stand. I think I've exhausted my luck in Atlantic City. I'm going to give myself a couple of months to find a job, then go out before I start to work. I'd like some sun and a little rest before I start reinventing myself."

"You've got friends in Vegas. We'll see that you have everything you need. You won't be on your own. And don't forget, anything you need, you know."

Jake rose and touched my chin lightly, underscoring his last words.

"It'll all work out," he said. "You'll see, one way or another. Just don't worry so much. Bonnie will be able to play to her heart's content, now that you're coming. Yes, indeed, Bonnie really outdid herself this time. She picked me a winner. Original people are rarer than works of art and I happen to know the price of quality is high in both cases."

Jake excused himself to make a phone call. I'd had too much champagne and wasn't sure of his message. His manner contradicted his words, but he seemed to be offering me something. Instinct advised me that if this were so, he would want a great deal in return.

Marco reappeared with Jake. "I'm sorry to end the evening, Lily, but I've got to leave the airport at dawn. Marco will see you to your room."

My suspicions vanished. I had been imagining things. Although I wanted to return to the casino, I was too tired. Marco escorted me to my room and said goodnight with a new touch of formality.

I lay still in the dark room for a long time, until the voices and pictures of the day's events stopped and the reality of my position asserted itself.

Although I'd come far, it was a journey I'd never thought to embark upon. The safe warmth was far behind me. I was out in the wilderness, forced to struggle and find my own way own way.

I was awed by the vastness of the freedom that lay before me, an Arctic expanse of aloneness. I felt icy blasts from the frozen tundra of the land I had so desperately coveted and won.

CHAPTER TWELVE

S taying on in Atlantic City for two days, I survived on chili, chocolate bars and black coffee laced with brandy, distancing myself from both past and future, getting lost in the cards.

Allowing myself a thousand dollars to play, I won and lost it a dozen times. Waiting until I was almost tapped out, down to the last hundred, I'd perform the high-wire act of winning it all back, a dazzling feat requiring ferocious nerve and feral tenacity.

During those two days, I spoke only to Annie. In a world of fantasy, resentful of obligations, I grew anxious if there was a line to use the ladies' room. My compulsion to play was so strong that I could hardly wait while the dealer shuffled the cards. At the end of two days, I was in a state of total exhaustion and my clothes hung on my body.

Checking out at noon, I left my bags with the bellman, determined to catch a bus. But as the day wore on, the idea of arriving at the Port Authority at some awful hour grew more and more daunting. At about two in the morning, I was ahead five hundred dollars. I hired a limousine.

I had played for fifteen hours straight, and my muscles were stiff and cramped, my voice hoarse from endless cigarettes. I was very hungry. The bellman whisked me into the back of a white stretch limousine, where I found pillows and a blanket.

The driver, a plump young woman dressed in chauffeur's livery, drove to an all-night stand on the outskirts of the city by the boardwalk. I dozed in the back as she went in search of food and returned with a feast of cheese-dogs, a delicacy of the South Jersey shore -- a hot-dog encased in deep-fried cheese batter. Opening the car doors, we picnicked in the early hours of the morning. The sea wind and the food revived me. We chatted as if we'd been friends for years and were accustomed to ending the night this way.

People who work in gambling resorts have seen everything. No quirk of personality or eccentric behavior is too bizarre. I smoked a joint, lay back on my makeshift bed and talked of life, love and gambling as the car sped across New Jersey in the black, starless night.

The driver, Bella, told the story of a prominent man living on a grand estate in Westchester whose addiction to gambling grew over the space of two years. His wife left him and his children became estranged, but he continued to siphon money from his business until he was forced to sell at a great loss. He gambled the rest of his money away, and now lived in the streets of Atlantic City, sleeping in a protected corner of the bus station. None of her stories had a happy ending.

I arrived home just before dawn, a crumpled, rumpled mess, and slept like the dead for twenty-four hours. I awoke, looking as if I'd gone through a major operation, drawn and pale, with swollen eyes, my head and body still cramped and sore.

Paul was away on a business trip for three weeks. When he returned we were cordial but distant, determined to keep the peace. Selena and Kitty came home the following weekend and we told them about our separation. The children sat on the sofa, cats on laps, faces ravaged, a family portrait of grief. We listed all the benefits, assuring them that it was better for everyone, that it was a trial separation. The question of divorce was held in abeyance.

"We're not a family anymore," Selena wailed. Kitty and Annie joined her, keening the bitter message late into the night.

After the agony of the weekend, the two older girls returned to school and, for the next two weeks, Paul sorted, packed and prepared to leave. Although he took few objects, the apartment had a forlorn and empty look. Annie and I were out the day the movers came.

*   *   *

The next morning, I awoke very early feeling elated. It was a perfect May day -- hot, bright and breezy. I flew into the park and ran faster and farther than I'd ever run before. Reaching the great lawn, I was dripping with sweat, spent and exhilarated. I turned cartwheels under the sprinklers, collapsing on the wet grass and gazing up at the blue sky.

On the following day the arduous process of looking for work was begun. I called anyone that might be of assistance. Paul and I had kept to ourselves for the last couple of years and it was difficult to call friends, explaining our present status, a world removed from the wealth and extravagance that had marked our former life. Fueled by need, I pressed on, looking for something that would lead to work.

Everyone was cordial but wary. No one had any ideas worth pursuing. I'd been idle for too long. My contemporaries had either been working for years or had gone back to school, supported by their husbands. The lack of experience cut short conversations with agencies, ads and companies. I began to feel I'd wasted the past sixteen years.

Only one call seemed to hold promise: a man I'd met in the casino suggested I deal blackjack at his after-hours place. There were jobs available anytime; I had only to call when I was ready to start. I filed that prospect in the back of my mind under last resorts.

In the midst of my search, Johnny called. He was at JFK, on his way to South America. Filled with himself, he rattled on about his powerhouse agent, his tour, his new Maserati. Before I could fill him in on my own life, the loudspeaker announced his flight.

I envisioned him boarding the plane, monogrammed Italian luggage in hand, flashing a snappy smile to the stewardess, his bright, roving eye surveying the plane's female population. Getting off the phone, I screamed with envy and hatred.

One of the rare job interviews granted to me was arranged by a playwright friend. I met with an independent film producer to discuss the possibility of working as a script editor. Lyle Plante was clever and successful. He was also, in show biz argot, a class act. It was instantly apparent that he had no work for me and had seen me simply as a courtesy to his friend.

"This is a difficult field, Mrs. Jarman," he said. "You're up against tough competition. The studios with offices in New York are filled with bright, aggressive twenty-five-year-olds who are happy to work fifteen hours a day for very little money. They have no family responsibilities. All their energy goes into climbing up the ladder."

His words were harsh but true. Though he spoke to me in the kindest terms, I couldn't help wish we were discussing someone else's career.

Then, after a moment's thought, he said, "Too bad you don't write."

"I did once," I said, surprised.

"What kind of stuff?"

"Short stories, poems. I started to write a novel once but I haven't touched it for a long time."

"Have you ever submitted your work to an agent or publisher?"

"No."

"Why?"

"I don't know. It seemed too ambitious. The pleasure of writing was sufficient compensation."

"Is it any good?"

"I suppose some things might be. But of course they need a lot of work."

"Writing is rewriting, Mrs. Jarman."

"I'd do anything, really."

"Then go home and read the novel again. If you feel you've got something viable, edit several chapters and submit them to a publisher or agent. If it's any good, there's a chance you'll get an advance to finish the book. It's your best shot."

"Writing a novel takes a long time. I need money now."

"If that's the case, you'll just have to write faster. Hunger is the best inspiration and you can always write while you work at something else. The best writers have had other, full-time work. Trollope, who wrote over forty-seven novels, wrote from five to eight in the morning, and then put in a full day at the post office."

"Yes, it's possible. I told a friend the very same thing a few weeks ago."

"You'll be starting what could be a real career. It depends upon how much you want it. There's one thing I know after a lifetime's experience -- you can get what you want, provided you want it desperately enough."

"Yes, but it'll be difficult to begin again after all this time."

"Haven't you ever gambled, Mrs. Jarman?"

"Yes."

"You'll be gambling on yourself by writing and finishing the book."

"The real question is whether I have any talent. In gambling all you need is luck."

"The chief requirement for any endeavor is luck, my dear," he said. I thanked him and left his elegantly appointed office, and his Meissen cups, confused and excited. I continued my job search but the ensuing interviews were curt and futile.

Finally, having exhausted friends and acquaintances, it became clear that I couldn't even aspire to an ill-paying job. Nick called to check progress. I mentioned Lyle Plante's idea that I rewrite my novel and submit several chapters.

"That could be your answer, Lily," Nick said.

"Do you really think so, Nick?'"

"Yes, of course. In the light of what I know about you and your life, it seems an inspired suggestion."

"I'll have to go through all of my work."

"When you're looking, if you come across a story or a poem that seems right for the magazine, send it to me."

"Your magazine is for young writers. Surely that's an additional category for which I need not apply."

"We publish new writers of any age. Besides, Lily, you have the youngest heart of anyone I know."

The conversation with Nick elated me and I began to dream of writing again.

* * *

Our anniversary fell on a hot day in June. I hadn't seen Paul since he moved out of the apartment, but we spoke on the phone frequently. We seemed unable to relinquish our roles: sounding boards, partners, references, memory banks, pillars, lovers, superegos, the best of friends, truest of allies, man and wife. The time apart had released us from our positions of mortal combat. We were free to be friends again.

After long deliberation, we decided to spend our anniversary together. We chose a restaurant in the theater district with no tender associations. Arriving early, I was seated at a table in the rear. Time passed slowly. I became restless, scanning every face. Finally Paul arrived, twenty minutes late.

I saw him cross the room and caught my breath. He was, at once, the intimate husband and the beautiful stranger.

He kissed me lightly, and for a split second our hands clasped.

"I hope you haven't been waiting long. I was tired and had to go the gym."

"I've been waiting for twenty minutes," I said in a tone angrier than I intended.

"Relax, Lily. Let's have a pleasant dinner. You wouldn't growl if I were a date, would you?"

"Sorry, Paul. Happy anniversary."

"Happy anniversary, my dear. You know, I think we'll keep on meeting for these occasions no matter what happens between us -- even if we're on our third marriage. You'd insist on it, wouldn't you, Lily?"

"Of course," I said.

"It's good to see you."

"Yes," I said, my eyes filling with tears.

"What's the matter, Lily?"

"Nothing."

"It's what you wanted, isn't it?"

"Yes."

"Why are you crying then?"

"It's not the way I planned to celebrate our wedding anniversary."

I had had another vision: friends, family, children, and toasts, cutting a cake, celebrating all the years together. I'd wanted to grow old with Paul, wishing for all the richness of a long, married life.

He was silent as my tears fell. Then he reached over and took my hand.

"It's the martini," I said. "You know I can't drink them."

"I know," he said. "You were always were a cheap drunk, Lily."

I dried my tears. "How do you like living alone?"

Paul waited before answering. His mind seemed elsewhere and he jotted a note on the small, leather-bound pad he always kept in his breast pocket. He lit my cigarette with a heavy gold lighter I'd given him years before, the twin of the one he gave me early in our marriage. He lifted his glass with a hand familiar to me as my own. I waited patiently, accustomed to his preoccupations.

"I love living alone," he said.

"That's wonderful." I said, feeling appalled.

"It's a relief," he went on, "and peaceful. I'm amazed that everything remains in its place each day. In the morning I leave a magazine on a table and it's still there when I return at night. Nobody uses my razor or my clothes. Everything's in its place."

"Women?" I asked, in spite of myself.

"You're really impossible, Lily," he said with a broad grin. I guessed that that aspect of his life had returned to normal.

"Are you jealous?" he asked.

"No, just curious," I said.

"Is there a man in your life?"

"No."

"I may have been sick, Lily, but I certainly haven't been blind. There's been somebody these past few years. There were too many clues -- flimsy excuses, hang-up calls, wrong numbers, unaccounted-for hours, nights that you came home too late and exhausted.

"Oh, Paul."

"No, Lily, I knew there was someone else. I hoped that he was good to you and made you happy. I'm deeply grateful to you, Lily, for your standing by me during these past years. I appreciate all you've done and I know what it cost you in emotional coin. But now that we're separated you must understand that I want to be with a woman. If you're alone, it won't be for long. You're too desirable."

"It's different for women. There are simply too many of us," I said. "But I'm sure you'll have no trouble."

"Right again, Lily," he said, smiling.

"Don't tell me, I don't want to know," I said.

"I'm not anxious to hear of your adventures either. Let's keep the whole subject off limits."

After that, the dinner was cozy and chatty, but I was conscious of a great irony. My concern had been that Paul was suffering and yearning to come home. His patent contentment and adjustment was infuriating. "Are you working?" I asked.

"I'm putting a land deal together and following every lead. It'll be a while before I make money. Meanwhile I'm using the money from the lawsuit for business and living expenses. You should have enough from your last win to keep you and the kids going, at least until things turn around for me."

"Take care of yourself, Paul. Get on your feet. I'll manage the rest."

"And you don't lose that money," he said.

"God, look who's telling me to stop gambling."

"Calm down, Lily."

I told him about my plan to go to Vegas. He agreed to have Annie stay with him if she didn't remain at the beach with her friend. I recounted my interview with Lyle Plante and his idea of my submitting edited chapters of a novel to a publisher.

"I've been telling you to do that for years. You always ignored me. When you started the novel, I told you to take it to a publisher. You worked away for years and then filed the stuff. Now some hotshot producer tells you to give it to a publisher and all of a sudden it's the right move!

"Every time I read a story or a chapter of the book and told you I loved it, you hid it from view, never to be seen again."

"I wasn't ready to listen before."

" Lily, going to Vegas is dangerous. You'll piss all the money away. Let me remind you, there's nothing to fall back on this time."

"I could deal blackjack at an after-hours place and write during the day," I said.

"What an idea! I can't believe you'd even consider it for a minute. All the kids need now is for you to be hauled off to jail! Who do you think you are, Belle Starr?"

He reached over and touched my cheek lightly.

"Old Paint," he said, calling me by a pet name which referred to all the battles we'd fought together through the years. "Don't worry so much, give yourself a rest. It'll work out."

"I hope so. And you, Paul, please try."

"I promise you that I'll do everything humanly possible."

"I know you will. I'm just tense tonight. I hadn't imagined this would be so difficult."

"It's hard for me, too."

"I'm glad it's worked out -- your living alone."

"It was right to move for everyone. I should have left long ago. It's a relief to be alone. I'm free to behave as I wish. There's no one to see me. The worst part was watching everyone watching me suffer all the time."

"Let's take a walk," I said.

"Come up to my apartment, Lily."

"That's not a good idea."

"It's small, but very nice. Like our first one. Nice and neat."

"It's been a tough night. Some other time maybe."

Having been his wife for so long, I couldn't easily fall into the role of mistress. Leaving the restaurant, he hugged me to him with a familiar sexual impatience. We walked up Broadway holding hands and stopped to browse in a bookstore, our favorite way to end an evening. Later, as we strolled past his house, he said, "I often look uptown, to where you all are."

Paul hailed a cab and dropped me off at my apartment building. For a long moment we stood on the pavement, looking at one another. Our eyes held the same silent wonder, at the strangeness of parting late at night to sleep alone.

Running to the top of the stairs, I turned for a last look. He was already in the cab, lost to view. Then, he moved forward and looked up at me, still there. Suddenly, a smile of radiant purity and beauty lit his face, and I remembered the first time I ever saw him, all those years before, when the brilliance of his smile, illuminated my world.

CHAPTER THIRTEEN

The apartment was silent and dark. Kitty and Selena were backpacking and Annie was at the beach. I'd be spending the night alone.

Abandoned that morning, Annie's room already seemed part of her past. Like the uncorked bottle of evaporated cologne, which lay discarded on her bureau, the quick present had become memory.

Sad and in danger of becoming morose, I impulsively took a ladder and climbed to the highest shelf of a closet. Cartons of writing lay neatly labeled. The novel was as I'd left it three years earlier when I'd begun my affair with Johnny. The pages were stiff and discolored with age.

I read until I fell asleep. Waking early, strangely energized, I went for a run in the park. Upon returning, I improvised an office in the old maid's room. Using a table for a desk, an odd kitchen chair, a makeshift lamp, I settled into my cozy aerie and worked all day. I read the novel several times and made notes.

After a sandwich for dinner, I fell into bed and was asleep before ten. During the ensuing days, I followed the same pattern:

running, writing, calisthenics and early to bed. Unaccustomed to work, it was difficult to concentrate. Daily running increased my acuteness and endurance. I'd begun to train for the long haul.

On the fifth day, my critical faculties sharper, it was clear that I could not continue to write the book I'd begun five years earlier. The story no longer had immediacy and relevance for me. Over the past few months, an idea had been forming itself in my unconscious, and now my long-dormant imagination erupted with the violence of an earthquake, pushing up layers of soil, silt and stone. Moving with a decisiveness that astonished me, I began the first chapter of a new novel.

That same afternoon, I had a fortuitous call from Annie. She was staying away another week. I called Bonnie and postponed the trip to Las Vegas until later in the month.

Having no interest in socializing, I spoke to few friends, using the answering machine in case the girls wanted to reach me. In those long morning runs, heart and mind leaping in anticipation of the day, I felt a happiness I'd never known. My desire to write was becoming stronger each day.

There were moments when I felt the book was already written and needed only to be committed to paper. I worked quickly, writing longhand on yellow pads, not editing or rereading, allowing the story to pour forth. At the end of the first week, I had finished one chapter and begun another.

Annie's return did not affect my ability to work. In the days preceding my departure for Las Vegas, I discovered, to my delight that one corner of my mind was always engaged in the book, which was swiftly becoming the focal point for everything. I was pregnant with it and its presence in my life had assumed the greatest reality.

One morning in the park, I ran into Phil McPhee, a writer whose forte was the third-rate scripting of second-rate media celebrities' lives. He earned vast sums of money by trivializing the trivial without achieving the distinction of great trash.

We talked about our lives and when I told him of my new venture he turned a scowl on me.

"You'll never finish the book, mark my words, never," he said.

I was astonished at his reaction since it was not in character with his habitual role of jolly party drunk. I later mentioned the meeting to Ronald Stark, the playwright who first sent me to Lyle Plante. He laughed, remarking that hacks with talent for the easy buck and none for the written word are invariably jealous and spiteful. Ronald exhorted me to write daily.

Another putative friend whose soft-core pornographic books enjoyed a wild success was personally outraged at my presumption. Audrey Remberg had come to her writing career late in life through the offices of a series of husbands, accomplished journeyman writers who harbored no illusions concerning their literary powers.

The moment Audrey assumed the mantle of author; she began to refer to her Craft, her Mentors, and her Duty to Her Readers. Newly divorced, she was engaged in capturing the roving affections of a married movie producer, having decided that credits on the silver screen were her destiny. Audrey approached writing in the same fashion she dealt with her duties as hostess. Queen of the canapé, doyenne of the hors d'oeuvre, she invariably had several trays in her oven. So it was with her books. She outlined copiously, delegating the actual writing to a team of hired hacks.

When I told Audrey that I'd begun to write a novel and was hoping for an advance from a publisher, her voice throbbed with concern, like a social worker.

"You haven't written in years, Lily, and there couldn't be a worse time for a first novel. The publishing world is in terrible straights."

"Just like the rest of the world," I said.

"It's impossible to publish a first novel now," she said.

"Your first novel was published at an inauspicious moment," I said.

"I was lucky," she said piously, choosing to forget that her good fortune consisted in no small part of having a cousin who was editor-in-chief at a publishing house.

"Then I'll have to be lucky too," I said.

"My book hit the heart of the reading public, Lily."

Her magnum opus had concerned itself with the romantic adventures of a homicidal maniac.

"We're not ambitious in the same way, Audrey," I said.

"You won't make a penny, even if you manage to find a publisher. It's a very long shot."

"I'll tell you a story of a long shot, Audrey. My grandmother came to this country with her illegitimate daughter and a friend's child, and the clothes on her back. She was illiterate, spoke no English, had no job, no money, no family or friends, no art and no craft. Walking the streets of the city, she found a job as a cook, raised her family and lived a long, rich life.

"And you, Audrey, would've told her that the situation was impossible -- the world was in terrible straits and she had no chance of making it -- that it was a very long shot.

"Because of my grandmother's courage, I began life with great advantages, and if I've got her DNA, then my shot's not so very long -- shorter by light years than hers."

*　*　*

I left for Las Vegas on a sunny June morning. I'd been writing with an intensity that left little time for thinking about the trip. It was not until I was on the way to the airport, crossing the Triboro Bridge, the sun sparkling on the river in the early morning, that I felt the first shiver of fear and excitement. My stake in the future lay there in the desert, to be won or lost in a single trial of effort. Like the Knight Errant, I felt the plane was my steed and my right hand, my lance. I was off to wrest the prize of a new life.

On the plane, I wrote twice my daily allotment. The story had come alive and in two or three months, I'd have several edited chapters. At that point I planned to avail myself of Lyle Plante's offer to take the manuscript to a publisher.

In the suffocating heat of the June desert at noon, Las Vegas looked like a famous beauty seen in the bright wattage of the morning after a long, hard night: shrunken and dusty. The native architecture, slabs of glitter supported by statues of naked Gods, had already been done in Miami Beach.

In the dim, cold oasis, I was greeted with a mixture of western warmth and over-solicitous amiability, shown into a room of sybaritic splendor, guaranteed to turn the hottest passion into giggles. A huge round bed was under a mirrored ceiling. A raised marble bath, large enough for a legion, had steps leading down. A profusion of gold and silver ornaments -- vases, lamps, urns -- filled the room. Roman style chaises abounded.

"The Royal Revel Tower," the bellman announced. "Ring for anything you want, twenty-four hours a day."

"I should've come here sooner," I said.

"It's never too late," he said. "Life's what you make it."

"Is that so?" I said, falling back my New York, wise-ass style.

"You're the master of your fate."

The room was filled with fruit baskets, champagne, chocolates and flowers with a card signed, "The Management."

"You must be somebody," said the bellman. "All those gifts -- and you're at the very top. This is the Pleasure Dome."

Shades of Coleridge shuddered audibly as the phone rang.

"Is there anything you desire?" a female voice aspirated into the phone. "Are you comfortable, Mrs. Jarman, is everything just as you wish?"

I assured her I was truly happy in every way, and she sighed contentedly, her day's work accomplished.

Rather than throw myself onto the tables fatigued and anxious, I decided to defer everything and bask in the sun, bridging the gap between New York and Las Vegas. I changed into a bikini and a sundress. Just as I reached the door, the phone rang. It was Johnny. My heart flew into my mouth.

"What happened to you?" he demanded. "Where have you been?"

"My plans changed."

"I kept calling and always got the machine. I didn't want to leave a message in case anyone else picked it up. Why didn't you call me?"

"I don't know. I didn't think it would matter."

"How come you're ten days late?"

"I'll tell you when I see you. I was just on my way out."

"When did you get here?"

"Twenty minutes ago. I was headed for the pool."

"You gotta be kidding! Get your ass over here right now. Suite twelve hundred."

Gone was my calm. I obeyed the imperative voice and rushed madly, once again passion's plaything. Heart pounding, I threw things into a bag, fixed my makeup, perfumed, powdered, brushed. When I reached Johnny's suite he was on the phone.

"Yeah, that's great, let's go with the deal. Sign it, get it down on paper. Yeah, baby, I love it. I love you, baby. Bye."

His face was smiling and tender as he turned to me. "I've got my first movie," he said, reverently. "It's a small but terrific part, and I get to sing the title song."

Suddenly, he leapt up from the chair. "I'm gonna be a fuckin' movie star! And I negotiated the deal, not my ass-hole agent. Me. I got everything! Salary, percentage of the gross, living expenses, promo extras, trips to the coast for her and all the kids. You name it, I got it."

"That's a big move for you," I said.

"Yeah, it's a chance for the real big stuff. Of course I'll keep the rest going; records, concerts, clubs and TV. You can never tell. It may not work out."

"You won't ever have to go back and work in your uncle's shoe repair store in Brooklyn, right?"

"Right," he said, embracing me. "You look great, baby. What kept you in New York?"

"I've begun to write a novel," I said. "That's why I stayed at home. The kids were away and I had a block of time to work quietly."

"Is that the same book you were writing when I met you?" he asked.

"This is a new novel. I've finished almost two chapters."

"What's it about?"

"Desperate measures."

"Just don't put me in your book. Nobody based on me."

"Don't worry, Johnny, no character will bear any resemblance to you. They're all literate."

"I want to see it when it's finished," he said. "Maybe it could be a vehicle for me -- a movie."

"I don't think so, Johnny."

The phone rang. As he listened his face darkened. "No," he shouted. "I said no, it's out of the question. Don't bother me again. Lay off me. I'm performing tonight! I can't deal with this shit on a day that I've got to sing! When I say no, it's no!"

"Who was that?" I asked.

"Her," he said. "Oh, I forgot to tell you the big news. We're moving into the city, a coop on Fifth Avenue, views, terraces, the works."

"You'll be across the park," I said.

"Yeah, too close for comfort."

"We don't have to see each other if you feel that way."

"That's not the point. I want to see you but I've got to be free. Not like before. Things have changed. My life's taken off. I know if I'm living in the city, you're gonna' crowd me. You want everything. You never know when to lay off."

"You mean that you don't want to pretend to be faithful to me."

"I don't want to explain myself to anybody. Not to you and not to her." He got up and glared down at time. "If the movie's a hit, I'll be living in Los Angeles most of the time, anyway. Besides, you've got to get your life going now. You've got to hustle."

"I know," I said. "I can't be in this position with you, Johnny. It's humiliating and debilitating."

"I'll call you. If you're free, okay, we'll see each other, and if not, that's okay too."

"I hate your offer. I refuse it. Absolutely."

"Don't be stupid. We've got a great thing going, babe. You just don't own me."

"I don't even have a short-term lease."

"It's the only way that's going to work for my life now. I can't be tied up the way we were before."

"I'm too old to be one of your girls, Johnny. Maybe it was always that way but I believed it was different. I may not have anyone in my life again but I certainly don't want to share anymore."

"That cuts out married men."

"Yes."

"You're nuts to give this up."

"And you're greedy and selfish."

"You always try to make me into someone else."

"Damn right."

"Everybody's married. You'll wind up alone. With nobody."

"Don't worry about me."

"You want me to leave my wife!"

"Leave her? When were you ever with her?"

The phone rang. I was relieved since our argument was getting dirty. Johnny spoke briefly and hung up.

"They've called a meeting about the show. I don't know how long it'll be, but I'll leave a message and catch up with you later. How are you fixed for cash?" he asked, attempting reconciliation. "I can let you have a couple of hundred, what with the deal and all."

"Oh, Johnny."

"Yeah, well, maybe I can let you have a thousand, if you really need it," he said, mistaking my reaction.

"I don't need your money," I said.

"Got to run, baby, we'll talk later."

He embraced me quickly. I was furious with myself for not having obeyed my instincts.

*   *   *

The enormous aquamarine pool glistened brilliantly under blazing sunlight. Oiled bodies lay prone on rubber rafts, eyes covered with dark glasses, arms rowing lazily. Artfully prostrate on chaises rows of bodies lay draped, arched, elongated, muscled, toned and jeweled.

The scene could have been titled "Gods at Play." Almost all of the bodies were beautiful. They ranged in color from pink and gold to darkest brown. I looked like a member of an alien species, a weary, city albino, beached on this island of bronzed bodies.

The intense heat hit the pavement and formed thick shimmering vapors of air, stunning everyone into total silence. There were no human voices. All that could be heard was the low buzzing of transistors, like sounds of interplanetary life.

I hadn't been on my chaise a minute before the sunlight attacked my body with an intensity that made me gasp and jump into the pool. How could all the other bodies remain so still, impervious to the dazzling, laser-like rays?

Gradually, the heat became more tolerable, acting as an invisible masseuse, obviating tensions, until I too lay ministered and painted by the sun. Joining the rowers in the pool, I was rocked and cradled by the water, unconscious of everything except the benison of the heat and the lizard-like instinct to lie unprotected under the sun.

Enveloped in a languid sensuality, I interrupted the heat with cold showers. When I rose to leave, my skin was deep pink, my limbs syrupy and soft. Returning to the room, I bathed in the marble tub.

Afterwards I fell into a heavy sleep, waking five hours later. My skin was burnished and glowing. I was tranquilized, distanced from everything, drifting on a smooth current. I had cast off the world to prepare for battle.

On the huge, lewd-looking bed, under the mirrored ceiling, I supped on dates, figs and cheese gleaned from the welcome baskets. I glanced up at my reflection -- one-shouldered white dress, bare arms ringed with golden bracelets, sandaled feet. Having tapped into the collective unconscious of the ancient deities, I had entered into a cosmic synchronicity.

I could have been a woman preparing to attend the festival of the Summer Solstice on a hot June night on the azure shores of Herculaneum a thousand years ago. I thought of the clever tricks, improbable disguises, capricious rewards and punishments of the Gods, and I wondered what mischief they were preparing for this night.

Stilled in body and soul, strangely at peace, I gazed over the lascivious Las Vegas night, glittering and pulsating with lights. The signs and symbols of gambling illuminated and beckoned.

And above, anointing the city, a sky of celestial splendor, midnight blue, with loose, swiftly floating clouds and beyond, the steely stars and a full silver moon.

Before descending, I murmured a swift prayer and closed the door on the insinuating rings of the phone, which I could hear even when I reached the elevator.

The casino was enormous, and glitzier even than the one in Atlantic City. From every niche, statued Gods stared at the crowds.

I watched the play without thought or plan, emptying myself, getting caught up in the mesmerizing, seductive movement of the cards, until I felt weightless. When I fell into the space where time did not exist, I knew I'd truly arrived in Las Vegas.

In Atlantic City, high-stakes players tended to segregate at high-minimum tables. But in Vegas, a man in jeans bet five dollars while next to him, a bejeweled Japanese woman played the limit of three thousand on each hand. Oblivious to one another, they could have been playing on opposite ends of the planet.

Choosing a low-minimum table, I started to warm up, not watching the run of the cards, playing by rote, shaking out the kinks and the terror, getting rid of the bad luck.

Drifting through the hours, I won and lost the same fifty dollars again and again. One of the men at the table was engaged in a running commentary in Swedish with someone standing behind my chair who I could not see. His gleeful laughter punctuated the conversation. The man behind me said something amusing and his friend rocked with laughter. I tilted back my head and caught his eye. He laughed down from a great height, his face a blur of tan skin and white teeth.

For a moment he moved to the side and I looked into a face wreathed in smiles. So powerful was his merriment that it reached through my state of near somnolence and I laughed out loud. It was the first sound I'd made in hours.

I doubled my bet and won, receiving a brava from my territorial protector as he proceeded to bemoan my losses and cheer my wins. When I rose to stretch he invited me to have a drink. I followed him through the crowd to a dark bar in the center of the casino.

Erik Nilsson, an architect from Stockholm, was tall, with blond hair turning gray and blue eyes smudged with exhaustion. Even in repose, his face was touched with irony and humor. He was with a group of business associates, entertaining clients while trying to survive with no sleep and holiday spirits. His group had visited seven cities in as many days. I remarked that it was a shame that he had to rush through the trip.

"I take things as I find them," he said, appropriate wisdom under the circumstances.

His English was excellent, his smile ravishing. After several drinks he suggested a walk near the pool.

The scented desert night was a miracle of beauty. Unsullied by gambling, I was calm and attuned to the world, grateful to be out of the casino. If I'd been alone, I would have knelt in a prostration of relief and joy just for being alive.

Climbing up a stone stairway to a narrow parapet we looked at the lights of city and sky, and embraced in the ineffable sweetness of the moment.

"I saw you at the pool this afternoon," he said. "You were enjoying the sun."

"The sun makes me happy," I said.

"I love it too. We do not have this heat in Sweden. When it does get warm, it's only for a very short time."

"That must be why Swedes always seem so sad"

"It's because we have such short summers."

"You're not sad, Erik."

"I have learned to find my summers elsewhere," he said.

We strolled around the pool, resting on a chaise, holding hands. Erik reminded me of my first lover, years before, in Spain, when I was seventeen. Nils had been Swedish too; a beautiful, gentle Viking, the perfect first lover.

There are those men who elicit a tension from women, images of a gauntlet thrown, a baring of weapons, a battlefield. Their attitudes arouse defense and struggle. But Nils, and now Erik, evoked the delicious sensation of falling on feathers.

"Come with me," he said.

I struggled briefly with the paraphernalia of responsibility.

"How do I know you're not an ax murderer?" I said.

"I'll show you," he said, pulling me up.

Back inside the casino, Erik propelled me to the safety deposit boxes where he retrieved his valuables. He showed me a passport, credit cards, work identification, a special delivery letter from his office, business cards. At the bottom lay a plastic horseshoe with a child's printing in Swedish.

"It's from my youngest daughter, for luck. Are you satisfied now?"

"You could've stolen these," I said.

He grabbed my arm and maneuvered through the crowd, walking for what seemed miles. Then up a long stairway to a room on the mezzanine. The sign on the door was the same as the name on Erik's business cards.

"I want you to see for yourself and be very sure," he said. The door swung open. There was a long table with about twenty men at the end of a gala dinner. Cigar smoke and raucous laughter filled the room.

Everyone had drunk a great deal and we were greeted with bellows of laughter, whistles and catcalls. Erik introduced me as a hotel representative, which brought a moment of decorum. I attempted to assess the proceedings under the guise of tour consultant. Erik's name was called repeatedly. His friend who had played at the blackjack table smiled and winked at me, remarking that Erik should bring back more representatives.

We closed the door and I turned to Erik.

"Okay, you win."

"We both win," he said, hugging me. "Do you have any more worries?"

"Actually, I'm concerned about your early toilet training," I said. "Nordic types have a reputation for excessive tidiness. Sex isn't tidy."

"So that's what you want -- messy sex?"

"Yes."

We sprinted down the corridor to a room, which was short on mirrors but had the largest bed I'd ever seen.

"Did you request the orgy special?" I asked.

"It's Empire size, as in Roman."

Turning off the air-conditioner, he opened the door to the balcony. While he set about lighting the hurricane lamps and opening the wine, I called the operator for messages. There was one from Johnny asking for a return call and one from Marco. The latter I took to be a summons from Jake.

I was bemused by my reluctance to return Johnny's call, to see Jake or even gamble. I wanted to stop time, to hold back the moment of engagement. And now, on this balcony overlooking Las Vegas, I was at last doing what I had yearned to do. I was getting lost.

Erik brought me a glass of cold wine. We leaned back in our chairs, arms stretched wide, as if on a sailboat, with the wind at our back. We were running free, on an oceanic swell of excitement.

Erik rose and came to where I sat and knelt at my feet. With a motion grave and sensuous, he lifted my leg to his lips and kissed the instep of my foot. The pressure of his lips on my skin exploded through my body like a bullet of pleasure. I knew that this night would need no art of seduction, only the burning energy to fuel the magnetism which had snapped us together.

Offering me a gift beyond compare, he said, "We have the whole night before us,"

In that instant, the movement of time altered, became the slow beat of desire, intensifying perception, deepening pleasure. He undressed me, and I felt the smooth weight of his hands, the sculptured shape of his lips as he kissed my shoulders. He loosed my hair and the sinuous coil caressed my back, stained with sun. Naked under the full moon, enveloped in a lustrous sensuality, we embraced.

Erik carried me to the bed. I watched him move, marveling at his beauty and grace, the shape of his head, the strong column of his throat, the long curve of his thigh. The limned lines of his body glimmered gold in the candlelight.

He removed a medal from his neck and then laid his smooth golden body over mine. The sudden surprise of exquisite flesh and we were caught in the current of passion, the other skin, the other breath, the primitive other we are forever seeking.

"I want to make love to you so that you'll remember this night always." he said.

And in our wild abandon, we entered into the eternal dance of time where nothing is forgotten, exulting in our moment until the chilled desert breezes dried our moist and heated bodies and brought through the windows the blood-red rays of the dawn.

CHAPTER FOURTEEN

returned to my room in the late morning. As I entered, the phone rang.

"Where the hell have you been?" Johnny demanded.

"Out on the town, sightseeing," I said. "I took a grand tour of the strip, came back and played in the casino all night. I just got in."

"I left a message for you at about eleven and another at two-thirty in the morning. How come you never called me back?"

"I never got any messages."

"Who were you with last night?"

"I was alone."

"Sure."

"I just got here yesterday. Who do you think I am, Johnny Messina?"

"Sometimes I wonder. How come you didn't call me last night, anyway?"

"I wasn't sure it was safe. I didn't know if your wife was planning a visit."

"You've called before when it wasn't cool."

"I'm smarter now. I've learned a lot from you."

"Yeah. Too much."

"I've had lessons from the master. Besides, my darling, how could I be with anyone else when you're nearby?"

"Too true," he said, with a whoop of laughter. "Well, baby, you messed up. I'm busy today and tonight with promos, publicity meetings and rehearsals. I won't be able to see you till tomorrow. Call me in my suite after midnight."

It was delightful to deceive Johnny. A year ago, I could never have done it, it would have been unthinkable -- but now I tasted the first pleasures of revenge, and they were remarkably sweet.

I showered, dressed in loose pants and a shirt, and filled my bag with cigarettes, mints, chocolate, a couple of joints and cologne. Included also was my new lucky charm -- a round, silvered stone worn by wind and sand.

"A memento of the desert," Erik had said when we parted.

Ravenously hungry, I went to the coffee shop and ordered eggs, bacon, pancakes and coffee.

"Looks like you're going in for the kill," remarked a man at the adjoining table. "Or you've had a very heavy night."

"Right on both counts," I said.

We chatted for a while. Carlos was a pit boss who had worked in Vegas casinos for twenty years. Surprised that I was alone, he offered his services to make my stay in Vegas comfortable.

"I can arrange for anything," he said.

Could he arrange for me to win? He admitted that he couldn't provide that particular service. But he knew of a very old, very rich man who would appreciate the company of a beautiful woman and would offer a great deal of money for the favor.

I turned down the offer, but Carlos quickly had another suggestion. It was a waste for me to be alone when there was a young, handsome pool attendant anxious to escort a beautiful lady for some reasonable recompense, silk shirt, gold cuff links or a lavish dinner.

Clearly everything was for sale. Carlos communicated this simply, without ambiguities, euphemisms, shock or smirks. He told me where I might find him if I changed my mind or needed another form of satisfaction.

After breakfast, strolling through the casino, I stopped to watch a player at a table cordoned off for privacy. One of the fabled Texans, wearing a Stetson, boots and using a Southern drawl, was playing two hands against the dealer. The thousand-dollar chips in front of him numbered about three hundred. He was betting five thousand dollars on each hand, and the pit bosses and armed guards stood watch over him, keeping sightseers at bay. During the shuffle, I asked and received the Texan's permission to watch him play.

Although surrender rules were then in effect, the cowboy didn't deign to use them. He gambled the corner off the cards, sixteen against a dealer's ace, fifteen against a ten, all sure-fire losses for him. It was an all or nothing battle and he wasn't concerned with economy. Playing with an utter lack of affect, the Texan kept his face impassive, not responding to wins and losses. He could have been playing dominoes with an aging relative.

Within minutes, all the chips were gone. His moment ended, the Texan rose, turned quickly and melted into the crowd. Another anonymous cowboy with a Stetson.

A witness, awed and outraged by the fortune squandered in moments, repeatedly told the story to anyone who would listen. A dealer standing idly by at an empty table told me this was not the real Vegas. It was the Vegas of June, a dead time. I found myself missing Atlantic City, the common language, the familiar faces, the street-wise talk, the feeling of school-yard heroics, the shared excitement of winning and the philosophical bitterness of defeat. This was not my part of the world. I felt as much a stranger as if I'd landed in a remote part of the Amazon. But then, everyone seemed to be a stranger in Vegas. Alienation was part of our trial by desert heat.

I took a marker for two thousand dollars and chose a middle position instead of my usual third-base seat. It had the psychological advantage of setting me up as a recipient rather than the dealer's challenger or the stalwart leader of the table. I was laying back.

I'd been in Vegas one full day and hadn't really played yet. My hand shook when I touched the chips. If I hadn't eaten a large breakfast, I would have fluttered off the chair like a piece of paper. Even before the first card was dealt, I was breathing heavily with my hands sweating and my fingers strangely heavy. I could barely light a cigarette. The casino was icy, but drops of sweat formed at my neck. The cards took on a strange cast, like a Tarot deck, transmitting messages greater than their intrinsic value.

My hands were good. Pat twenties, natural splits and doubles against the dealer's weak hands, and still he pulled the magic cards and I lost. The two-thousand-dollar marker was gone in minutes. I felt a wave of nausea and dizziness and was unable to continue playing. I made my way back to my room. Ignoring the message light on the phone I threw off my clothes, told the operator to hold my calls, got into bed and fell asleep instantly.

The message light blinking in the darkness awakened me at seven-thirty. I'd slept for five hours. There was a message from Johnny. Tomorrow night was definite. And there was another message from Marco, which I returned. The phone was answered by a butler announcing Jake Berman's residence. Marco was calling at Jake's behest to invite me to dinner at the ranch. It was already late, the guests had been there for a while, but he could pick me up in half an hour. Jake would hold dinner for me.

I accepted the invitation, grateful to leave the casino. I bathed, dressed quickly and when I reached the hotel entrance, Marco was sitting in the back of a silver Mercedes limousine with the license plate JB 1.

"Did they get you, Lily?" Marco asked.

"What makes you say that?"

"Your voice on the telephone," he said. "And now the look on your face."

"It's nothing to worry about," I said, "Let's not talk about gambling."

Marco handed me a brandy. Drinking it, I felt better immediately and leaned back in the air-conditioned splendor as we drove in total silence through black roads under a sky covered with stars. Eventually we arrived at a pair of black wrought-iron gates with J and B outlined in gold. Security guards led by leashed dogs checked our names against a list before showing us entry. Then we drove up a long, winding drive for about ten minutes, past another security building and several more armed men, including two on horseback.

The massive walnut doors of the house were initialed in turquoise stone. There was no mistaking the owner of this property. The ranch was adobe, a long low series of white buildings whose lights reached out into the darkness.

A butler dressed western style, jeans, jacket and boots, led us into a huge space broken down into levels and areas. At the far end, people were seated on low couches in front of a stone fireplace. The furniture was oversized leather. Navajo rugs of rare beauty covered the terra-cotta floor. The colors were mute, only the desert plants and flowers blooming with color. To the right of the fireplace, a Picasso woman exploded into the room.

Bonnie, acting as Jake's hostess, introduced me to the group. Pamela Morris, an actress on a popular television series, had begun her career as a dancer in Las Vegas and had returned to star in a show for several weeks. Richard Morris, her husband, a pretty-faced former actor, presently managed his wife's career.

Terry Roberts, a slight, intense writer of message movies, seemed to be the group's token intellectual. Sid was mixing Margaritas.

"I'm happy to see you here, Lily," Jake said, kissing my cheek.

In his native habitat, Jake seemed larger, more substantial. The splendor of his ranch flattered him, like good movie light. He looked rich and important. We dined soon after and I was seated on his right, the place of honor. Everyone knew each other well and the conversation was show-biz talk, that circular, boring rehash of what everyone present already knew, prologue to the real point: the recital of the guests' latest career gambits.

Pamela Morris lowered her voice to divulge the top- secret news. A perfume was to be named for the character she played in the television series. She tossed back her mane of platinum curls, adopting the pose of an astonished gazelle that didn't know how she had strayed from the herd and become famous. She bore the weight of her success bravely and believed that interest in every aspect of her life was evidence of a high level of artistic temperament.

Implicit in the conversation was the dirtiness of the business, which all the guests faced with *noblesse oblige,* sullying themselves for the sake of art and self-expression. They were like priests assigned to work in a brothel, but guarding still the sacred flame of true religion and the high seriousness of their calling.

I was clearly of no importance in that great world. Blissfully ignored, I was free to enjoy the food and wine and bask in the aura of cool, expensive beauty. An exquisite crystal chandelier hung above a very Old Italian refectory table covered with English silver. A Degas sculpture was in a niche carved in a wall.

"You've finally smartened up, babe," Bonnie whispered in passing. "This is the table to play. Only winners here. You won't be sorry you came."

After dinner Richard Morris and Jake left the group for about ten minutes, walking out to smoke cigars. When they rejoined us in the study, Richard was assuring Jake that whatever he'd agreed to was simple to arrange. "No sweat, Jake. It's a pleasure for us, believe me," he said, breaking into his first real smile of the evening.

Jake was a gracious and unpretentious host. He suggested a short tour of the house, leading us through huge rooms filled with a treasure of modern paintings, beautifully hung and lit. His latest acquisition, a Georgia O'Keefe of a vast flower, imposed its carnal beauty over a desert landscape. As the others walked on, I remained, willing myself into the cool surface of leaf and petal, until I could almost touch the yellow edge of the flower. Engrossed, I suddenly heard the hissing voice of Richard Morris coming from behind a large Coromandel screen.

"I gave my word to Jake," he said.

"You had no right," his wife answered, furious.

"It's a fortune of money."

"I won't touch it, you bastard," she said.

"There's no way I'm going to stay in Vegas another minute. I worked like an animal for years to get out of this sleazy, fuckin' town. I hate it here. I signed on for this act because you threatened and hassled me for weeks. You wore me down. I didn't want to fight you any more. But you swore it was only for three weeks. I've finished serving my time and I'm leaving day after tomorrow. My movie starts rehearsal in a week."

"And I say you'll do five weeks more here," Richard said, in a menacing voice. "I gave Jake my word. There's no way I'm gonna renege on him. People fall all over themselves to do him favors. He asked me for this one. He doesn't ask unless it's important. It's not a good idea to refuse Jake Berman. Don't forget that, ever."

"I'm not staying," said Pamela.

"The money's great. What are you complaining about? You're getting shit money for the movie."

"But it's a movie, asshole! Not a TV show or a club act, its a major motion picture. The ratings on the series aren't so hot anymore -- it's not going to last forever. A movie will give me exposure. I need that. It's the right move for me. And that's what I care about, my career."

"You'll get another offer," he said.

"I waited two years for this one."

"You're getting fifty-thousand dollars a week for five weeks. That's a quarter of a million dollars for showing your ass."

"You lousy sneak, you can't use me that way. I know what you've done. You've gambled away a fortune, run up markers you can't meet. That's it, you've lost a bundle and I've got to pay the piper, right? You weasel."

"Bitch," he snarled. Then there was the sound of shuffling feet, a slap and a stifled cry.

"Pull yourself together, quick. I heard somebody," Richard said,

Slowly, I began to understand. Jake's power and position alone were not sufficient to claim the obsequiousness I had observed. There was an additional element that gave him supreme power. The thread that bound Bonnie to Jake was the same one that pulled Richard Morris's strings. He was a gambler and like Bonnie, protected by Jake in exchange for certain favors. The sinister quality of their enslavement was clear: like the junkie, the gambler's greatest allegiance was to his vice.

I took my time getting back to the study. When I arrived, everyone was saying good-bye. Marco had disappeared. In minutes, Jake and I were alone.

"You should see the colors of the landscape in the daylight, Lily. The views are beautiful," he said, handing me a brandy. "I hope you'll stay long enough for me to show you the horses. I'll have the other wings open too. There are acres of beauties."

"I'd love to see them," I said. "The ranch is perfect, it's an extraordinary place to live, an Eden."

"It's true. I have everything but the right woman to share my treasures. Believe me Lily, I get very lonely. Of course, there are women, for a night or a weekend, but beyond that, it gets very difficult. My wife spoiled me. I'm too particular. Like everything else, finding the right woman is a matter of luck. The right place at the right time."

"A door swinging open magically, a fortuitous turn of the head."

"Or someone walking into a restaurant," he said, smiling into my eyes.

"I felt that when you sat down at the table in Atlantic City."

"It's nostalgia, Jake. I remind you of your youth and the old neighborhood."

"The kid from Brooklyn," he said.

"You still see me as a kid?"

"Yes," he said. "I hope you stay that way. It's part of your charm, Lily."

"That's too bad, Jake. I'm determined to grow up."

"What have you been doing in your quest for adulthood?"

"I'm looking for work. I've begun to write a novel."

"Oh, really, that's interesting. Have you written before?"

"Yes, but now it's different. I have a real commitment to it."

"How will you manage working day and night?"

"I'll find a way. I can always get a job as a waitress."

"That's very ambitious."

"I've been asleep for twenty years. I have to make up for lost time."

"You're asking too much of yourself."

"Don't you demand a great deal of yourself? I'm certain that when you began your career you worked night and day, and still do."

"There are other alternatives for a beautiful, desirable woman, Lily."

I turned and stared at him. "What do you mean?" I asked.

"You'd have no trouble finding someone to finance your future," he said.

"I've already done that. It didn't work. There are no free futures. One never learns to live if someone else takes responsibility."

"That was your marriage. You're out of it now. There are other ways."

"Such as what?" I asked.

"I'll be frank with you, Lily. I'm very attracted to you. You must be aware of my feelings so this won't come as a surprise. I'd like you to come and stay here with me for a week. Instead of knocking yourself out trying to make it in the casino, I promise that you'll leave with enough to finance the completion of your novel. Or whatever amount you've got in mind. You could write without holding down another job. It's a better answer than blackjack. It's a sure thing."

"I couldn't do that, Jake."

"You say you've wasted twenty years. What's another week? Stay here with me and I'll make it worth your while, for your future, too."

"I'm not sure I understand," I said.

"I'm interested in seeing how we get on together. Not only for a week. I'm not getting any younger. I want a real love affair with a woman again. And I'm not ruling out marriage. You appeal to me, I feel at home with you, and I think I could live with you. You're the first person I've met who makes me happy in same way as my wife. Maybe that's possible for me again."

I poured myself a glass of water and drank it quickly. "I'm sorry, Jake, I can't do that," I said, turning back to him. "I'm still married and I don't feel that way about you."

"Love comes later for some."

"I can't accept your money."

"You mean you'd rather kill yourself on the tables than take it easy here?"

"Yes."

"You're not using your freedom and independence in the right way, Lily."

"Have you always made the right choices and lived your life without mistakes? The point is to take responsibility and start making mistakes."

"You don't take responsibility by gambling. The owner wins. You see this ranch, this art collection, and these houses. I'm a very rich man. I have all the money because the house always wins, Lily. That's the law -- here in the desert and everywhere there are casinos. The last time I gave this speech was ten years ago, and I never intended to use it again. You're a babe-in-the-woods."

"You've just finished telling me how much you like that quality in me," I said, tartly.

He pulled me up out of my chair and kissed me passionately, holding me close to him, breathless with ardor, his fingers trembling as he touched my face.

"I haven't felt like this about a woman in years, Lily. Let me help you. It will make us happy. I have everything to give you."

I felt nothing, no stirring of passion, no response, only embarrassment and shock at the sound of genuine emotion in his voice. I'd expected anything but this.

"I want you very much," he said.

I groped for a simple fast way out, cursing my stupidity, knowing that I'd brought this upon myself. What had I expected? Why did I never think? What was I doing in this palatial ranch; locked in a passionate embrace with a man I cared nothing for?

The answer, when it came, revolted me. I was here for the same reasons as the others; I wanted his protection and his money. But in no way did I want Jake.

Freeing myself from his grip, I fled to the bathroom and stayed there for a long time. Instinctively wiping his kisses from my mouth, I was repulsed by my own self-deceit. I'd said the right things to Jake, but deep down, it *was* his money that had fascinated me from the first moment.

I had no illusions about what I'd do to survive if all else failed. But I had not yet arrived at the point of last chances. I'd struggled too hard to escape the doll's house merely to change owners. I had no illusions about Jake's requirements in a woman. I'd be satellite to his star, quickly reduced to ashes by his burning power.

Get your ass out of here, girl, my silent soul advised me. I hadn't fought Paul's tyranny to become an object in someone else's bedroom, no matter how lavishly appointed. If I was going to be fucked over, I'd do it in my own style.

Returning to the study, I was relieved to find Jake on the phone, his feet up on the desk, a smile on his face, engrossed in a conversation. I drank brandy and admired the room, which had its replica in the Atlantic City hotel suite where I'd last seen him. The only apparent difference was the landscape painting over the mantle.

When he hung up, Jake seemed revitalized. The romantic moment had vanished.

"What are you going to do, Lily?" he asked.

"I'm afraid I have to refuse both your offer and your advice."

"You could've had it so easy," he said. "I don't understand you."

"I've done it that way before. It just looks easy."

"You're choosing something impossibly hard. I don't only mean gambling, but the way you'll have to live, alone, without choices."

"It's the only way I'll ever call my soul my own."

"Are you hooked on gambling, Lily, or do you really think it's your only chance?"

"I'm not hooked, Jake. I've begun to hate and dread it."

"You've got some money. Take it and leave."

"It's not enough. I started to play today but I became so frightened I had to run. I escaped into sleep."

"You've every right to be scared. It's very risky."

"The nature of business is risk, making money is risky. You didn't get from a tenement in Williamsburg to this desert palace by playing it safe, having someone dole out money to you. I want to be somewhere that I got to *myself*. I have to reach for something, take a path somewhere."

"What do you want ultimately, Lily? Where do you want to get to?"

"I want to be the supreme commander of my life. I want the power that men have always had over their destiny. I want to be boss."

"You're going to need courage and tenacity."

"The manly virtues?"

"Yes, if you like. But then you'll be like a man, tough, ruthless and driven. Those are not nice qualities in a woman."

"That's another risk I'll have to take. I look forward to developing my masculine potential. I come from a long line of tough women. That quality hasn't surfaced yet, but then I've never been tested. One of my great-grandmothers rode bareback into her eighties and another caught mice with her hands. I call that tough."

"You're right about that, Lily," he laughed. "What's your blackjack game plan?"

"I have to double my winnings. It's my only real chance. I've got to take it."

"Don't drag it out like a slow death, Lily. Go in and do it quickly."

"Like an assassination?"

"If you like give yourself a time limit, two or three sessions and get it over fast. You can play for hours or days waiting for the right shoe. Since you don't count cards, you'll piss away everything just staying in the game. Playing itself, is very expensive and debilitating, especially if you're playing with scared money."

"That sounds like good advice."

Jake glanced at his watch.

"Marco will see you back to the hotel, Lily."

I was surprised at his abrupt dismissal. He now seemed anxious to get rid of me.

"I'm sorry about tonight, Jake."

"There's no need to be sorry, Lily, things just didn't work out, that's all." He came over and put his arm lightly on my shoulders. "You're preoccupied and burdened. Another time, another place, things might've been different. They still might be different. You've got my phone number and I've got yours. Keep in touch. If you need anything, call me."

Marco arrived and I said good-bye. Before we left the room he was back on the phone. It struck me then that I had apologized to him for not accepting his offer. He should have been apologizing to me for his crude, egotistical proposition.

Marco and I waited at the front door for the limousine when suddenly a silver sports car careened into the driveway. I saw Pamela Morris's platinum blond tresses emerge. She was alone and hurried into a small side door, which opened at her approach as if she'd been expected. My night's replacement. *Sic transit gloria mundi.*

My vanity suffered a brief shock. Naively, I had thought Jake sincere. Perhaps he had been, for the moment, which in Vegas can be eternity.

My last thought before sleep was the painful realization that I had not been truly horrified by Jake's suggestion that I play the whore. I had felt outrage but I had lied to myself. Although I had quickly rejected his offer the moment it was uttered, it had become a real possibility.

I'd been gazing over the abyss too long. Jake was right. I had to get out fast.

CHAPTER FIFTEEN

The balcony doors had been left ajar and the night breezes had become the leaden heat of noon. I showered, drank two icy cokes in lieu of breakfast and wrote for three hours. Coming upon a moment of true illumination in the novel, I felt happy and lucky, the perfect mood for gambling.

I left my room and headed downstairs. The time had come to face what I had been avoiding since I arrived in Las Vegas. I resolved to take Jake's advice and limit my play to several short sessions.

The dealers stood at empty tables, arms folded, waiting for the start of another Saturday night. It was early enough to play head-to-head without interruption, but I quickly discarded that idea. Too risky. When I had begun to gamble, I had moved on instinct, but now I knew too much. The excitement would inevitably lead to excess.

Turning a corner, I ran into Bonnie. She had just stopped playing. I fell into step with her and we went to the main lobby and sat down on opposite couches. She lit a cigarette with trembling fingers. She looked devastated.

"I lost too much, even for me," she said, taking a few deep drags. "There's no way I can find this kind of money. Sid mustn't get wind of this."

"I'm sorry, Bonnie," I said.

She put her head between her hands. "How was last night?" she asked.

"Fine."

"Did you get something going with Jake?"

"No."

"Why not?"

"I'm not interested in Jake, Bonnie."

"Alice in Wonderland!" she said, raising her head. "You don't have two nickels to rub together, Lily. Wake up! Jake could give you everything. He had me invite you out in the first place."

"I didn't imagine that this junket was dependent upon my going to bed with Jake."

"The junkets are a matter of hotel policy. The special treatment, a room in the Pleasure Dome is for very high rollers."

"I'm betting my life. I don't know how much higher you can go."

"So what happened?"

"He offered me money to stay at the ranch for a week. I refused."

"It never hurts to be nice, Lily. Screwing someone for a week is no big deal. It's the way life works. Was he mad when you left?"

"We parted on friendly terms. He even asked me to keep in touch. I've still got his private number."

"That's a laugh, Lily. You've got yesterday's private number. Today, there's a different one. You'll never get through."

Bonnie's face hardened. She had obviously tested the number recently with no success.

"I'm afraid I've made things awkward for you, Bonnie, but Jake wanted too much for his money."

"Don't be so fuckin' superior with me, Lily."

"Oh, Bonnie," I said, taken aback.

She closed her eyes and took a deep breath. "Forgive me, Lily. I'm crazy now. I lost too much."

She was pale and still. It occurred to me that her shadow was not around.

"Where's Marco?"

"Like the money -- gone," she said bitterly. "I've got to make some calls fast. How long will you be around?"

"A few hours."

"You're scared to play, Lily. That's why you haven't been at the tables for your usual fifteen-hour stretch."

"Yes, I'm scared. I want to get it over for good."

"If you can," she said.

"This is the end of my casino career, Bonnie."

"We'll see," she said, taking a compact from her purse and examining her face closely. "What a ruin I'm becoming. This life makes you old fast. All that recycled air, coffee, adrenaline, stress, and cigarettes -- three, four packs a day. And the real killers: scrounging, lying, cheating, humiliation."

There was no mention of cocaine and booze. She patted her face with powder. I saw there was a streak of dirt under a chipped red fingernail.

"I wish you'd shown up earlier, Lily. Maybe you would've distracted me or pulled me away from the table."

"That's an impossible thing to ask of anyone, Bonnie. No one can get you up and away from gambling."

"You're right, Lily. I'm strung out. I know it wouldn't have made any difference. How long are you going to stay in Vegas?"

"I'm getting out as soon as I can. It feels like death here, I hate it. It gives me the creeps."

"It's no different from Atlantic City, Monte Carlo or Nassau. It's the capital of gambling, that's all. You can get out any time, nobody's keeping you prisoner. Just don't let me see you scrounging at a two-dollar table for supper or waiting to make ten bucks for a cab to the airport. Have you made any money since you hit Vegas?"

"I lost two-thousand dollars yesterday, but I haven't really played much."

"Too bad for both of us," said Bonnie. "You were my ace in the hole. I wanted to borrow from you."

I looked up, aghast. "I'm in no position to lend money," I said.

She scratched her neck and arms violently, raising small, red welts on her white skin.

"What's the matter?" I said.

"I need some snow."

"You look sick, Bonnie, I'll take you to your room." I was torn between pity and repulsion.

We got up to the suite and Bonnie did several quick lines of cocaine. She felt shaky and asked me to stay with her while she bathed. Her fine-boned dancer's body was covered with red welts, bloody from scratching. After the bath, she did more coke. I didn't join her and refused her offer of a vial for later.

Very soon her spirits improved and she dressed and put on makeup. I waited for her in the living room while she made phone calls. She entered smiling, apparently successful in finding the money to cover her losses.

"I'm sorry I lashed out at you, Lily. I didn't mean to be so nasty. Please forgive me."

"Of course," I said.

"I wanted you to come to Vegas because I like you. I thought it would be great for you to become involved with Jake. I'll call you later and we'll have drinks or dinner. Good luck at the tables. Thanks for getting me up here."

It was eight o'clock when I called for my messages. There was one from Johnny putting off our date until ten, which meant I had two hours to play.

The encounter with Bonnie had disturbed me deeply. A curtain had been torn away allowing me a glimpse of her that I hadn't imagined. I felt sure that if I looked deeper, the revelations would be more appalling.

The casino was crowded now. I sat down at the first free seat, ordered a marker for five thousand dollars and began to play with five hundred in cash. While the cards were being shuffled, I reviewed my assets: cash, things to sell or hock, or borrow from. The bottom line. Then the first cards were dealt and the ride had begun.

I bet fifty dollars a shot and when my marker arrived I was up about two thousand dollars, the amount I'd lost the previous day. Now I alternated fifty and hundred-dollar bets. Watching every card, I tried to guess the number of face cards and aces. Several minutes of this simplistic counting left me confused and frustrated. I'd have to keep it simple and in Marco's words, "Be lucky."

I escalated to two-hundred-dollar bets and got a double-down hand, a ten against the dealer's nine. It was not a great double, but it was the designated play. For the first time I was tempted not to double but to play it safe. I checked myself, doubled and won.

Playing the indicated strategy for the game, I always split and doubled, never lowering the bet even if I was losing. I'd won big money through risk and now was certainly not the time to hesitate and play it safe. At the end of the shoe I was ahead two thousand dollars.

Three men at the table were totally absorbed in the play. There was a tacit silence. The dealer, taking his cue from the players, dealt swiftly. We were all there to do business. I was glad for the quiet formality of the group. There was no small talk, none of the usual requests for drinks, change or matches. When a girlfriend of one of the men came to the table, she was ignored. Players who wanted to socialize left quickly.

Everyone was betting high, five hundred and more. After the second shoe we were all ahead. The invisible shell around the table grew harder. One of the men played the empty slot, not wanting anyone to join the game and spoil what had become a winning team.

Sensing my moment had arrived; I escalated my bets to five hundred a hand. The shoe ended in a thrilling burst of winning and I was ahead seven thousand dollars.

I felt a sense of infinite possibility, a destiny fulfilled and the giddy power of creating that destiny. I was no longer at fate's mercy.

I now began to vary my bets, two-and five-hundred a clip, staying even, straddling the shoe, when suddenly at the crest, spinning with wild momentum, I pressed my bets into the thousands and ran head-long into the jagged glass wall of a losing streak. When the shoe ended I'd lost my five thousand marker and the seven-thousand I'd won. I felt as if my skin had been scraped off along with the chips. I changed tables.

Ordering a second marker for ten thousand, I started over. But the losing streak followed me. The cards became weapons, attacking me, wounding me, and there was no defense. I could do nothing right and I couldn't stop. Too anxious even to sit, I roamed from table to table, watching the run of the cards.

When the moment seemed propitious, I jumped into the middle of a shoe, attempting to steal someone else's luck. Once I stopped in the ladies' room and placed my wrists under the icy tap to revive myself, but I couldn't even feel the cold water. I glanced at someone's watch. It was nine forty-five. Johnny would have to wait.

It wasn't too late. No time to panic. I could still win. I'd lost only fifteen thousand dollars. I now had fifteen to make forty-five. All possible, still.

Choosing a dark corner, away from the glare, I ordered a marker for ten thousand dollars. I regretted now that I hadn't taken advantage of Bonnie's offer of cocaine. I ordered a double brandy and breathed deeply to fill my lungs with oxygen, but I was full of smoke and could only gasp and cough.

The brandy instantly blurred sensation and replenished courage. I'd play a few shoes more, then call Johnny. The marker arrived. The fresh stack of chips gave me the illusion that my money had been miraculously returned.

Gathering courage, I placed a five-hundred-dollar chip in the betting circle. I felt a curious sense of detachment, a lightness, as the dealer swooped and removed the chip. A second later I couldn't remember the cards.

I changed dealers, seats, and positions. I played two slots, then three slots. I couldn't win. What had once seemed a trick, a magically summoned gift, was now an impossible feat. I could not imagine that I'd ever won. Hand after hand, blow after blow, I played in a trance, watching myself being eviscerated. The more I lost, the higher I bet, attempting to recoup the money. The ten thousand vanished in minutes.

Moving to an empty table, I ordered a marker for five thousand dollars, requesting ten five-hundred-dollar chips. Playing head-to-head with the dealer, betting five hundred a hand, I lasted one shoe. When it was time for the last bet, I had two chips left. One thousand dollars. I looked at the dealer for a long moment. In his eyes I saw the pity and revulsion I'd felt for Bonnie.

And then the anesthetic was cruelly ripped from my face and I was flooded with pain. The full consciousness of my act was unbearable. I'd lost twenty-nine thousand dollars - all the money that stood between my family and disaster.

I got up and backed away from the table. My vision was blurred and my legs weakened. I made it to the elevator and back to the room, clutching a handkerchief to my mouth.

I hit the bathroom just in time and vomited in great waves. The bitter taste of gall was my punishment. For a long time I lay on the cold tiles in the slime of my own failure. Shock and horror flicked my consciousness on and off like a switch as the blackness engulfed me, swallowed me, and spat me back into life. There was no part of me that was not in agony. Muscles, nerves and skin were alive with torment. Turning on the taps full blast in the stall shower, I howled.

Cold. Hell isn't hot, it's cold. I've been there and I know. Life is warm and death is cold. Blinded by tears, tormented by the sound of my shrieking, I knew the void, the savage, remorseless cold. I had to keep moving or I would freeze to death.

Lifting my body, slowly, painfully, I got on all fours and crawled to the bed. Spasms of pain racked my body as if I'd been poisoned. Shivering, I wrapped myself in the bedclothes and wept.

At last I was released from the icy grip. I lay on the bed, bathed in my own effluvia and stared up at the mirrored ceiling: dress filthy, stained with vomit, matted hair face bloated with grief, smeared mascara blackening my eyes painted, gaping holes in my flesh.

Time became, like the pains of a first birth, immeasurable. My soul was rent with grief. A moment passed, and then another. I heard a ragged intake of breath, a cry. My own.

The phone rang. Moving painfully, I lifted the receiver and placed it on the pillow beside me.

"Where the fuck have you been?" Johnny screamed.

"Here."

"I've been waiting an hour! What happened to you?!"

"Can't talk."

"You lost! That's it! You fuckin' lost!"

"Yes."

"You fuckin' lost a lot of money!"

"Yes."

"You're a fuckin' addict. I told you to stay away from those tables. They killed you, didn't they."

"Yes."

"How much did you lose?"

"Too much."

"Everything?"

"Yes, yes, yes!"

"Jesus, you fucked up good. I knew this would happen. What are you going to do?"

"Can't think."

"What about him?"

"I've got to leave him out of this, he's just getting on his feet. He couldn't take it. I'll handle it alone."

"What about Berman, the rich guy? Did you connect with him? He's loaded."

"So?"

"You be nice to him. He'll be nice to you."

"I'll manage, Johnny. It's all right. You can get off the phone."

"You've got to be smart now. Use what you've got. You're a great-looking, sexy broad. That's what you've got, use it! Get what you need. You're down on your ass now. You have no choices. God, this is depressing. I can't have this in my life. I've gotta move on."

"Move on."

"What the fuck do you expect me to do?" he shouted.

"Nothing."

"You're not my responsibility."

"I never counted on you for anything."

"You're going to drive me crazy. My life's perfect now. Everything's coming in right. This is not good for me."

"Stop it, Johnny. Leave me alone."

"Do you have money to get home?" he asked.

"Yes."

"What are you going to do now?"

"I told you. I can't think."

"I mean about tonight. This was my only free night for weeks. It's too late for me to make other plans. I haven't had dinner yet."

"Sorry."

"You're in a bad way," he said accusingly. "You'll feel better after a shower. Relax, order some food. I can't stay on the phone. I gotta make some calls. I gotta run."

"Bye."

"God-damn it, you sound like you're dying."

"Be glad that I'm not dying in your bed."

"Bite your tongue," he said. "You know there's nothing I can do."

"That's clear."

"That's not what we were about," he said. "And this scene is depressing the fuckin' shit out of me. What a downer. I can't have this in my life. Even every once in a while, even on the phone. No more. It's not worth it. The whole thing is too messy. I can't touch it. Not anymore, not ever. This is it, kiddo, you really blew it this time."

He slammed down the phone and I put my receiver down on its cradle. A wave of spiritual nausea hit me. A blow upon a wound. All our passion, our high secrets, our play were reduced to ignominy.

The phone rang.

"Mommy," Annie cried. "I miss you so much."

"What's the matter, Annie?"

"I left a message and you didn't call me back."

"I never got it, darling. Why are you crying?"

"I had a fight with Amy. I came home early. Oh, Mommy!" Her voice broke. "When will you be home?"

"Tomorrow. I promise."

"You sound sick."

"I have a stomach ache."

"I love you, Mommy."

"Me too. How's everyone?"

"Fine," she said. "I'm at Daddy's. He's reading. Did you win?"

"A little. I'll see you tomorrow, darling."

I had yearned for the sound of Paul's voice. To have, just for an instant, his comfort and love to speed me on. But he could never know.

After speaking with Annie, I felt stronger. All those years as foot soldier in the army of mothers had instilled a second, innate sense of responses, which worked when all other systems broke down.

This system now took over, shutting off the waves of self-pity and grief, turning on an inner core of resilience and hope. I'd carried it off before. I could carry it off again. I would embrace responsibility as the spar it had always been and hold onto it, for dear life. It would hold me aloft through the hours, as the waves crashed over my head, spinning me, flinging me on the rocky shores of my life, cutting into the skin of my soul.

I walked out onto the balcony. Far below, the deep aquamarine glow of the pool drew me down. I put on a bathing suit and robe, and took the elevator to pool level. In the darkness, the warm water was voluptuous and smooth against my body. Floating on my back, I remembered another night, long ago, when I was sixteen working as a waitress in New Hampshire. One brilliant night in an icy New Hampshire lake, heavy with the scent of pine and honeysuckle, I stayed in the water after everyone returned to shore, floating, gazing up at the stars.

I was enraptured by the beauty of the night, the high romance of my solitary moment in that supreme instant of love for my own life.

In the casino pool, I swam slowly at first. Then I hit my stride and sliced hard through the aquamarine water, pulling myself forward, arms stroking, legs kicking, muscles flexing, heart pumping, lap after lap through the desert night. After a long time, totally spent, I stepped out in the cool air, the glow of racing blood warming me.

I returned to the room, showered, dressed and packed my bags. Walking through the casino, I was struck once more by its voracious, raucous carnival. It was four o'clock in the morning, but could just as well have been midnight or noon. In this world without clocks, time didn't exist. Memory was banished.

Quickly walking to the front desk, I checked out and took a cab to the airport. Reserving a seat on the first flight out of Vegas, I sat in the waiting room, watching the gradual shifting shades of darkness become a rainbow dawn blazing over the dark mountains.

The flight to New York would be leaving soon, and as I reached down into my voluminous travel bag, automatically checking for wallet, money and ticket, my hand fastened on a thick smooth leather case. I pulled it out and opened it. There were pages and pages covered with writing. It was the book. My book.

The flight was announced. I rose and walked across the tarmac onto the ramp of the plane. Climbing to the top, I paused to look at the brilliant dawn. The first rays of the sun lit the silver plane, radiating a warm, golden hail of light upon my face, upturned to receive the blessing.